*In his laboratory, Lord Darvey demonstrated
a procedure for Elizabeth . . .*

"Let me show you how different two specimens can be," he announced eagerly, preparing to repeat the operation. "Oh, drat!"

Somehow, his Lordship had missed his mark. The consequence was that a shower of lead shot rolled onto the table and from there every which way on the floor.

"Let me help you, my lord." Elizabeth hitched up her skirts a little and got on her knees beside him. She scooped up a fistful of shot, then tilted her head to look into his smoke-colored eyes, now more nearly on a level with hers.

Time seemed to slow and get slower. "The beads," she said stupidly, swaying toward him and holding out the shot.

"Yes." Lord Darvey sounded distracted, and there was a thin film above his upper lip which had not been there before. "No . . . I mean no, they aren't beads. Please stand up, Miss Hanley. I shall do so as well."

A SERIOUS PURSUIT

ELLEN RAWLINGS

DIAMOND BOOKS, NEW YORK

A SERIOUS PURSUIT

A Diamond Book / published by arrangement with
the author

PRINTING HISTORY
Diamond edition / January 1991

ISBN: 1-55773-451-8

Diamond Books are published by The Berkley Publishing
Group, 200 Madison Avenue, New York, New York 10016.
The name "DIAMOND" and its logo are trademarks
belonging to Charter Communications, Inc.

PRINTED IN THE UNITED STATES OF AMERICA

10   9   8   7   6   5   4   3   2   1

To Robert, whom I love

A SERIOUS PURSUIT

One

ELIZABETH HANLEY HAD barely set her feet on the top step of the worn old staircase when she heard the sounds of battle. At least she heard one sound that could be classified as martial. Her uncle was shouting at someone. "Wretch!" she heard upon drawing closer to Lord Beowulf's workroom. "Uncommon ingrate!"

It was not difficult to guess the recipient of these insults. Not a week went by that she did not find Uncle Beowulf and David, her twin, in noisy opposition. Although England's war with Napoleon had come to an end at last, the one between her uncle and David probably never would. Fortunately, she had grown so used to their skirmishes that most of the time she was able to ignore them.

She gave a tug to straighten the apron that covered her old brown round gown, then pushed wide the partly open oak door. As she had assumed, her two closest relatives were inside, glaring at each other with mutual loathing.

Her entrance did nothing to abate the hostilities. "Shut the door," Lord Beowulf ordered without turning his angry blue eyes from her brother.

Elizabeth did as she was bid, then walked around her short, corpulent uncle to stand beside David. She should be thankful, she thought, glancing up at the latter with some amusement, that the two men did not resemble each other except in the way they glowered. Of course, she had to admit, even though David was her twin, he did not look a great deal like her, either.

What physical resemblance there was lay mostly in the similarity of their coloring, both of them having green eyes, fair complexions, and hair the russet of autumn leaves. Those elements combined in David with his neat, straight features and lean look to create an image of self-confidence, even of arrogance. In contrast, Elizabeth's rounded, pretty face and lush mouth made her appear appealingly soft and agreeable.

This impression of complaisance in her, however, was not totally accurate. Although not as vocal or as fiery as her twin, she was his equal in independence. And, though neither would have considered it, she was probably much more sensible.

"What's amiss?" she asked her brother, ignoring Uncle Beowulf.

David waved one narrow hand at his adversary in a gesture of dismissal. "Uncle is being even more preposterous than usual. It's not for you to worry about, though, Liz. I'll take care of it."

"Take care of what?" she asked, blandly ignoring his directive. "Tell me what has brought you two to dagger drawing this time."

"Well might you wonder," said Lord Beowulf, looking at his niece without the slightest indication that he appreciated her manifold charms. "All I did was suggest that you render me a small favor—in return for what I've done for you and that . . . that. . . ."

"Wretch?" Elizabeth prompted wryly, speaking over David's loud objection. "Isn't that what I heard you call him just a minute since?"

Without a trace of embarrassment, his Lordship admitted it. "Indeed it was, and very apt, too, my dear. After all, it's not as though I want you to take on something that you aren't up to or that would overset you. Why, then, I ask you, should he kick up a dust?"

This speech, which unhappily left Elizabeth as much in the dark as she had been before, so enraged her brother that he began bellowing at the older man, who quickly responded in kind. "Stop," she ordered, the beginning of a headache making her feel less than her usual tolerant self; but her demand had no effect.

Her eyes darted around the cold, dreary room which had served as the nursery to earlier generations. Now, however, instead of being filled with the hobby horses and other paraphernalia of childhood, it was given óver to a motley assortment of furniture for storing the specimens and equipment his Lordship used in his experiments. Some of these materials were spread out on the stained wooden table next to her; they would have to do.

She pushed a yellowing skull and a container of mustard seed to the worn Turkey carpet. The squabbling stopped immediately, replaced on David's part by laughter.

His Lordship, however, clearly was not amused. "Elizabeth Hanley," he shrilled, his face turning as bright as his thinning red hair, "how could you?"

Awkwardly, he bent his portly frame in its ancient, tight green waistcoat and gathered up the skull; then, with as much care as though it were his baby, he restored it to its former place on the table.

David quickly insinuated himself between Elizabeth and their uncle in an attempt to draw Beowulf's fire. "Let me guess," he said, kicking with a scuffed old boot at a box clearly marked *Indians—Brazil* in which the skull had been shipped. "That came from one of the card-playing crowd at Brooks's, isn't that so?"

Elizabeth started to laugh, but she hastily brought herself under control. It wouldn't do to ruffle her uncle's feathers more than she already had. Besides, in the cause of her incipient headache, she didn't want to risk anything at present that might encourage her twin's insubordinate bent.

Not that it needed her encouragement, of course. As she knew full well, David would willingly have roasted their uncle with much less excuse. As he often told her, he considered Lord Beowulf's theories concerning his specimens silly at best, and, besides, his interests lay in a different direction. Though only two and twenty, he was their uncle's estate manager. It was a position which David very much enjoyed, although he hadn't originally opted for it.

Uncle Beowulf had set him to it, having seen an opportunity to get some use out of the willful nephew who, with his twin, had been foisted on him when the twins' parents had died five years past. His scheme having turned out so well with David, he'd dismissed his housekeeper and replaced her with his niece.

Unlike David, however, Elizabeth was not best pleased at her demotion to unpaid servant. She longed for a different, more fulfilling life.

With a sigh, she examined her uncle's face to see how well her twin's effort to deflect his wrath had succeeded. It was obvious that it hadn't at all, because Lord Beowulf now snapped at her, "I could make you sorry for what you did."

David moved nearer his uncle at these words and leaned one shoulder against a tall mahogany cabinet that stood between two windows. "I shouldn't threaten her if I were you," he advised with a coolly menacing smile. "Someone might take exception to it. Besides . . ." he stretched out his arm to let his hand trail slowly down the other man's rumpled shirt front, "it isn't good policy to use that tone when one wishes a favor."

"Just so." Uncle Beowulf looked up and smiled broadly.

"Not that I'd permit her to do it," David continued, wiping the smile away.

Elizabeth stamped her small foot in its flat-heeled slipper. "For the last time," she said impatiently, "what are you two talking about? Tell me at once or I shall leave this room."

"Let me." His Lordship forestalled his nephew's outburst. "I shall tell it. You may not credit this, Elizabeth, but there is an upstart in the world of natural philosophy!"

"Oh, no," she declaimed dramatically, to her brother's great enjoyment.

Not having a sense of humor himself, Lord Beowulf never recognized it in others. "Oh, yes," he assured her, earnestly thrusting out his chins, "it's true. He's someone who's been traveling through foreign lands for several years collecting skulls. Now that he's returned to this country, he means to make a name for himself in my speciality. In fact, so I've been told, he's had the audacity to apply to give my annual lecture at the Royal Society in April."

Though Elizabeth strove valiantly, this time she could not repress her mirth. It was several seconds before she recovered enough to ask her affronted uncle, "Who is this impudent vagabond, pray tell?"

His Lordship's face reflected his struggle over how to deal with his niece. The need to tell all being stronger than his sense of outrage, it won the day. "His name is Lord Darvey," he replied, forcing himself to sound affable, "but though he's impudent, indeed, still one must always be reluctant to call an earl a vagabond. Besides, he has a home in Grosvenor Square—has homes in several counties, in fact—not to mention a rent roll of at least thirty thousand a year."

Elizabeth tried to look suitably impressed at this evidence of Lord Darvey's value. "I withdraw the second half of my description," she said demurely, causing her brother to chuckle. "Still, it surprises me that such a wealthy man would not send someone younger to do his collecting for him."

"Why, what do you mean?" Lord Beowulf sounded indignant. "He is but thirty, young enough to see the whole world if he has a mind to; and, in fact," he added gloomily, "I think that is what he has done. According to my sources, Darvey has, his own self, amassed a collection representing nearly all of the continents."

Sighing heavily, his Lordship continued, "There you are, then. That's the sort of man I have to compete against—and what is so amusing now? I have not said anything humorous."

"Indeed, you have not," answered Elizabeth genially, her soft, rosy mouth curving upward. "You have said hardly anything at all beyond the fact that he is rich and travels. Don't you know anything particular about him?"

"Particular?" his Lordship repeated in a perplexed tone. "I've told you what his rent roll is. How much more particular can I get?"

Elizabeth rubbed a small, pink finger against a gouge in the long table. "Oh, with something more intimate, I suppose, such as whether he is married and has children or if he has interests other than collecting skulls."

Lord Beowulf looked shocked. "Collecting skulls is not an interest. It is a serious pursuit. As for those other things you mentioned, there is nothing to tell. Like me, he is a bachelor. And a good thing it is, too. If he had a wife, it might be harder for you to carry out my plan."

While his Lordship had been talking, David had mostly contented himself by standing by and grimacing to show his disapproval. But now he could contain himself no longer. "Carry out your plan, indeed. As I've already told you, she'll do no such thing. Come, Liz." He thrust out one fine-boned hand in an imperious gesture. "Let us return to our duties."

"Just a minute, you young hothead," admonished his Lordship. "If I ask her to help me, then that is her duty, and don't you forget it."

Elizabeth touched her brother's arm. "It's all right, David. Please don't regard it. Besides, I want to hear this famous plan."

"You're very wise, my dear," Lord Beowulf said almost benevolently. "Would that your brother were as sensible."

At that, David started to round on his detractor again, but

Elizabeth stopped him with an admonitory look; she'd had more than enough of their feuding this morning.

How she wished she could separate the two combatants permanently, she thought with a sigh, not to mention removing herself from her uncle's sphere. If only David could find a position somewhere else.

Unfortunately, deliverance did not seem imminent. No one would offer her brother a position as estate manager without a letter of recommendation, and that, despite his numerous promises to supply his nephew with a splendid one, Uncle Beowulf had thus far failed to provide.

It was the promise of that essential letter, rather than the hope that Beowulf would make David heir to his fortune, that kept them there. Beowulf had told them that he was leaving his money to the Society for the Purity of the English Race, an obscure organization that despised foreigners. Since that was just the sort of thing he *would* do, they had no reason to disbelieve him.

Elizabeth shrugged her slender shoulders. There was no use thinking about their situation now. She might as well get this discussion over with. "May we forego the incivility?" she said briskly. "I'm waiting to hear your plan, Uncle."

"Yes, yes," he approved. "Here it is. I'm sure you'll admire it." He stopped to clear his throat and then proceeded. "It's simple, really; that is what makes it so elegant. As anyone but your brother would acknowledge, it's imperative that I remain informed about what this Darvey creature is up to. You, my dear, will help me learn it."

Raising a fat, freckled hand to forestall his niece's remarks, he hurried on. "What I mean for you to do is move into the Grosvenor Square place as companion to his great aunt who lives with him so that you can send me the information I need. I think a report every few weeks should serve, don't you? Your brother can collect it when he goes up to London on my errands." He smiled happily. "There, you've heard the whole. If you still have questions, I'm ready to answer them."

Somewhere during this recital, Elizabeth's mouth had fallen open. Now she sputtered. "What? Did you really say what I think you said? Are you telling me that you wish me to remove myself to this person's house so that I can spy on him? I cannot believe it."

David bunched up his fists. "Not to mention your willingness to send your own niece off to be little better than a servant to some stranger, which doesn't seem to bother you one whit."

"I say, you needn't either of you put things like that." His Lordship busied himself kicking an unused lump of sea coal back into the fireplace whose flames barely took the chill off the room. "I'd merely like you to keep me *au courant*, Elizabeth, that is all. And as for being a servant, why, a companion isn't anything of the sort. Hers is a serious pursuit, just like mine."

"It's a shabby idea." Elizabeth made no effort to hide her scorn. "So there's no use trying to pretend it isn't, Uncle. And it's ridiculous, besides. What makes you think Lord Darvey's relative is in need of a companion, or would take me on if she were?" Not waiting for an answer, she added, "Are you sure that your brain hasn't gotten small?" Since his Lordship's major theory was that small brains were found only in inferior types, like women and other races, this was disparagement indeed.

His Lordship's florid face grew ruddier. "That will be enough of that sort of talk, or you'll find yourself in the cold. Do what I ask, however, and there might be something nice in it for you—a pretty agate necklace, perhaps? You females like to have things like that, don't you?"

The twins exchanged a disgusted look.

"As for my idea being impractical," their uncle continued without encouragement, "you needn't concern yourself there. My friend Cranley has it all arranged. You see, Darvey told him about the vexing problems he's having finding proper staff, including a companion for his great aunt. That's because of the lower classes' unreasoning prejudice against human remains—against Science itself, I might say. At any rate, Cranley offered to find a steady, sensible woman for Lady Treadway, and the offer was accepted. You, of course, shall be that woman. In fact," he added eagerly, "I'll send Cranley a note straight away telling him to let Darvey know that you are coming and to praise you to the skies; that will do the trick."

Raising his voice to drown out David's irate comments, he continued, "Once you have the position, you only need stay to gather information until Darvey reads his paper. That is but four months hence, hardly any time at all. To set your mind further at ease, let me point out that in the unlikely event Darvey discovers what you are doing, no harm can come from it. He'll merely have you dismissed and in a week's time forget you had ever lived in his house. Why, he could pass you on the street and it would not matter."

"Forget Elizabeth?" David's expression was incredulous. "Tell us another plumper, why don't you?"

Both men stared at their female relative, causing her to blush so that her creamy skin turned almost as scarlet as her very fetching mouth.

"He'll molest her," yelled David.

Uncle Beowulf looked truly shocked. "Natural philosophers never molest women. It's absolutely unheard of."

"You're mad," David gritted, "and I won't have it. We aren't staying to hear another word." Grabbing Elizabeth's hand, he began pulling her in the direction of the hall.

"Wait." She hooked one foot around the chipped leg of a faded, old wing chair to stop their exodus. "I'll do it." Disregarding her brother's short, rude remark, she added, "On condition, of course."

Lord Beowulf somehow managed to look elated and cautious at the same time. "What condition? I've already promised you a necklace."

"I don't want a necklace." Elizabeth's voice quivered with suppressed excitement. "I want your letter of recommendation. I want it to say that David is a fully competent estate manager who has served you well. Otherwise, I won't go."

"You won't go, anyway." Her twin glared at her. Not even the promise of the object he most longed for was enough to make him willing to give his approval.

Elizabeth ignored him. The opportunity presented, perhaps never to come their way again given their uncle's obvious disinclination to help them, must not be overlooked; it might well be their only chance to establish themselves.

Beowulf's next words confirmed her feelings. "Oh, well, as to that, we can discuss the letter when you come back. I'm sure we can reach some sort of accommodation then."

Her pale green eyes narrowed. "I'm sorry, but that just won't do. Unless I can have the letter first, I must decline."

She propped herself against the table and watched the tug of conflicting emotions reflected in her uncle's face. Despite his disagreements with David, he obviously did not want to lose his services. He probably would rather not lose hers permanently, either. His scheme was not quite so palatable now.

"If you don't remain until the very day of the lecture, the letter is forfeit," he hurled at her, whether to make the best bargain or because he no longer wished to encourage her compliance Elizabeth could not determine. "I want your word on that!"

What were a few short months in exchange for the opportunities freedom might bring? Elizabeth did not hesitate. "I swear it," she said.

Ignoring his extended hand, she put her arm through her brother's. Now she was ready to make her exit.

As soon as she and David were in the hall, he started to argue with her. She had known he would. She would have none of it, though, and shortly left him to go to her room.

Once there, she walked over to the bird cage that stood in the least drafty corner of her poorly heated bedroom. "How would you like to accompany me to London?" she addressed Primrose, her pet canary. "You can help me be a spy."

A small black eye stared at her.

Elizabeth put her face into her hands. "You're right," she said, speaking to the bird through her fingers. "What I'm about to do is unconscionable, and I should be ashamed. I *am* ashamed!

"But what other choice do I have? If I don't accept this opportunity, David and I will languish here until we expire; then Uncle will add *our* skulls to his collection."

The canary appeared to hesitate, then burst into impassioned song. "No, no, never say so," his guilty mistress cried. "I'll make amends to Lord Darvey somehow; you'll see. I give my word!"

"Well, are you ready to set off?" her uncle asked cheerfully the next morning when the two of them met at breakfast. "I sent a note to Cranley yesterday to tell him to inform Lord Darvey that you are coming."

Elizabeth looked at him with disbelief. "Surely, you aren't serious. I cannot leave now. There are a hundred things for me to attend to before I go. No." She raised her hand to stop him. "You will just have to contain yourself. If all goes smoothly, perhaps I can set off early next week. In the meantime, why don't you give me David's letter of recommendation?"

In a display of spleen, his Lordship threw down his napkin and pushed himself from the table. "You'll have to wait," said he. "You aren't the only one who's busy with a hundred things, you know."

Now left alone, Elizabeth quickly finished her meal and went to the village to seek someone to take over her household duties. This was no easy task since her uncle had long since alienated nearly everyone in the vicinity. Finally, however, she found a woman sufficiently in need of funds to be willing to tolerate him for four months.

Elizabeth spent the days following showing the new housekeeper what needed to be done. She also got her wardrobe in order. She washed and ironed all of her clothes and even refurbished some of her frocks and hats with bits of ribbon and old lace she found in the attics.

Truth to tell, hardly a thing looked any better when she finished. However, since their allowance from their uncle rarely stretched to providing them with new garments, there was nothing else to be done. Probably, she thought with a wry grin, she was not dressed well enough to pass herself off as a companion. How ironic if her uncle's clutchfisted nature kept her from carrying out his scheme.

In between her activities, Elizabeth again attempted to procure the promised letter. She was determined not to go off without it. Unfortunately, her uncle seemed equally determined not to provide it and made himself remarkably scarce every day.

He did not even join them in the dining room the evening before she was to leave. Instead, he sent the twins a note advising them to take their mutton without him because he meant to have a tray brought to him in his laboratory.

It was there that Elizabeth found him, bent over his worktable peering at a large skull with a perfect set of teeth. "Look at this specimen," he said without bothering to turn around. "Isn't it beautiful? It is skulls like this that make it all worthwhile."

When Elizabeth's only response to this enthusiastic if cryptic comment was to lift a delicate reddish brow, his Lordship added, "The seller told me that it came from an East Indian who died here, but I know that what he said cannot be true. It is too large. Being members of one of the inferior races, East Indians cannot have large skulls."

Elizabeth ignored his explanation. "I've come for David's letter. I need to have it now."

Her uncle widened his blue eyes in what he apparently considered a portrayal of innocence. "Letter? What letter? I don't know to what you're referring."

"The letter the lack of which will keep me from setting off tomorrow," replied Elizabeth, accompanying her words with a sardonic little smile.

"Oh, that letter." Unable to escape, his Lordship grudgingly put down the skull and walked with a heavy gait to his desk. "I did write one, just in case. . . . I'm sure it's here somewhere. Yes, here it is." He ran the single sheet of paper across one deeply creased palm, then reluctantly handed it over.

Elizabeth took it from him and perused its contents, which did not take long since there were only a few words on the page. "This will not do," she said upon finishing it, and returned it to its author. "You must write another."

"And what is wrong with it?" Lord Beowulf asked belligerently. "Myself, I think it is quite a good letter. Certainly, there is nothing in it to offend."

Elizabeth's green eyes bored accusingly into her uncle's guileful face. "I think you must mean there is nothing in it to commend. Tell me, what is the correct interpretation of 'I can recommend him without hesitation if you want that sort of a person'?"

"Why, what is there to object to in that? I said 'without hesitation,' didn't I? What more could you ask for? Oh, very well. If you insist upon being overnice about it, I'll make you another."

With that, his Lordship picked up his quill pen and set himself to work. Soon he provided a second letter which if not brimming with praise at least was worded strongly enough to be acceptable. "Thank you," said Elizabeth after reading it carefully. "I shall be certain to put it in a safe place so I need not trouble you over it again. And now I shall bid you good night, Uncle." Overlooking his scowl, she gave him a jaunty smile and went off to bed.

At first light the next day, she was in her uncle's ancient traveling carriage, her shabby portmanteau strapped to its roof, with Primrose in his pretty white cage beside her.

"You can still change your mind," said her obviously

unhappy brother who had come out to see her off. "All I need do is give Uncle back his letter." When Elizabeth shook her head, causing the new trimming to quiver on her unseasonable straw gypsy hat, he added with a confidence that both knew was unwarranted, "Since I'm certain to find a position eventually even without a letter, you really don't need to go through with this."

Elizabeth gave him a saucy grin. "Oh, yes I do. After what I've been put to in getting your testimonial, brother dear, I've earned it and mean for us to make use of it."

The grin changed to a reassuring smile. "Now, there's no reason for you to succumb to the dismals. Hasn't Uncle assured us that I will be safe? And as for being separated from each other, it won't be so bad. You'll see; this will come to an end before you know it." On that hopeful note, she took her leave.

How splendid if such optimism had endured the whole distance from Epsom to London, but, sadly, it was not to be. Elizabeth blamed her descent into the doldrums on the bleak, wintry landscape, with only some huddled sheep or a few horses standing near a leafless tree to enliven the scene. Or perhaps the cause of her malaise was that she had nothing to occupy her during the hours it took for her to reach her destination. Whatever the reason, the result was that she passed the time in fretting.

One of her concerns was the nature of the man to whose house she was going. She knew little enough about him despite her uncle's litany of dry facts, but she felt certain that he would be unpleasant. He was like Lord Beowulf in his fanatical devotion to natural philosophy, wasn't he? Surely, there would be other similarities as well.

She envisioned someone younger than her relative, of course, but equally short and squat. He was touching a skull with clammily affectionate fingers, as she'd seen Uncle Beowulf do so many times. Wincing, she closed her large green eyes.

Her gloomy reflections were at last cut off by the arrival

of the carriage at Lord Darvey's town house in Grosvenor Square. This was an impressive cream-colored building four bays wide. Her knees shaking a bit, Elizabeth, still clutching her bird cage, climbed two shallow steps to a shiny black door set off by a brass knocker.

She was admitted into a small, white entry hall. It led to an imposing black and white marble staircase hall beyond. Neither hall contained much in the way of furnishings or paintings.

A footman led her to a ground floor room closed off by tall double doors. He knocked and then stepped aside for Elizabeth to enter.

Her attention immediately focused upon the room's two occupants. At the same time, she realized that she was in a laboratory similar to her uncle's. Yet even her cursory glance revealed an order and neatness here far different from what she'd known in Lord Beowulf's house. Lord Darvey's specimens were set out neatly upon precisely aligned shelves. There wasn't even a box on the floor that David could have kicked if he'd accompanied her.

Which of the men before her was the one upon whom she'd been sent to spy? Neither seemed remotely like her uncle.

If she had to choose between them, she supposed she'd be forced to pick the rather untidy-looking blond man, although with his open, ingenuous face, so different from her uncle's, it was hard for her to think of his having any interest in common with Lord Beowulf.

Still, it could not possibly be the room's other inhabitant, the one with the dark hair and cool grey eyes. He had a tall, athletic figure and a handsome face, its narrow, high-bridged nose and clean profile reminiscent of those seen on Roman statuary. His clothes were beautifully tailored and, in Elizabeth's admittedly untutored opinion, the very epitome of uncluttered good taste. She could not conceive of anyone looking more unlike her uncle.

No, he could not possibly be part of any group that

included her uncle. He seemed too sane, and he was decidedly too good-looking.

Elizabeth flushed when she realized that the grey eyes were examining her quizzically. It was time for her to put a clamp on her run-away thoughts.

She addressed herself to the blond man. "I am Elizabeth Hanley, your Lordship, come to be your great aunt's companion if it pleases her." She capped her speech with a curtsy.

To be exact, she started to execute a curtsy. Somehow, however, Primrose's cage got in the way and caused the ordinarily sure-footed Elizabeth to lose her balance and sprawl upon the floor. The cage, which seemed to have taken on a life of its own, rocketed off. It left behind a trail of gravel and wispy yellow feathers to mark its course.

The blond-haired gentleman stared after it, transfixed. Not so the other spectator. His face expressionless save for a slight twitch at the corners of his lips, the tall, dark-haired man caught the flying bird cage expertly between his hands. Only then did he return his attention to its owner. "It's not necessary for you to fling yourself at our feet, you know," he said kindly. "The usual sort of greeting will do. Oh, and by the way, *I* am Lord Darvey."

Two

PUTTING DOWN THE bird cage, his Lordship extended a large, tanned hand to Elizabeth. "Up you go," he said, a hint of a smile tugging at his well-shaped mouth as he pulled her to her feet. "Any bones broken?"

Elizabeth was blushing so furiously that she felt as though liquid fire coursed under her skin. How could she have done that?

"Well?" He propped his long body gracefully against a glass-fronted cabinet and waited.

"I am fine, my lord. Thank you." She forced herself to look into his amused grey eyes, then said as calmly as she could manage, "I'd like to apologize for my awkwardness. I am not usually like that, and I do not know why it happened."

His Lordship glanced over at Primrose's cage. "I think your pet got in the way. What do you have in there, a vulture?"

Elizabeth had been so upset over her spill that she had actually forgotten about her beloved canary. Hurrying over to where his cage rested on the floor, she knelt and pulled up the quilted cover to peer at him. The bottom of his cage looked a dreadful mess, of course, but Primrose appeared to be unscathed.

When he saw her, he peeped forlornly, then hunched

down as though preparing for another disaster. "I think he's feeling undone," she said, accompanying her words with her bewitching, dimpled smile.

For an instant, his Lordship looked startled. Then the expression was wiped away as though it had never been. With a wave of his hand, he directed her to a large black leather wing chair. "This is my great aunt's nap time—Miss Hanley, isn't it?—so why don't you tell us about your qualifications, instead?"

Before she could begin, however, he pointed to his untidy companion and said, "This is my friend Mr. Eccleston, who is as interested as I in hearing about you."

"Indeed, I am," said that gentleman, his friendly blue eyes taking on a wary look. "Unless you're completely out of the usual mold, I doubt that you would care for it here. Darvey has all these skulls about, you know. Young women don't like them."

Obviously, thought Elizabeth, Mr. Eccleston did not like her. Her smile this time was perfunctory. "Oh, they do not bother me."

"Is that so?" His Lordship rubbed his index finger over a platinum chain that ended in a functional-looking pocket watch. "Tell me, do you feel that you would be content to spend your days with a very old lady who hardly ever leaves her room?"

Was he, too, trying to discourage her? Suppose he refused to give her the position? Lord Beowulf had been so certain that his friend Cranley's recommendation would be enough, they hadn't discussed the possibility that she might not be taken on.

She was certain her uncle would insist upon the return of his letter if she failed to get the post. Yet she could not bear to return it, not after having a chance for a decent life for herself and her twin within her grasp. She must not fail.

"I do not foresee any problems," she replied so decisively that Lord Darvey grinned openly this time. Having said that, however, she hesitated, realizing that she did not know what Lord Cranley had told his Lordship about her. He might have said that she'd spent her formative years entertaining two maiden ladies who never stepped out of their house, or he might have said she'd accompanied the local dasher on her numerous engagements. Since there was no way to find out, she would just have to take her chances. "I am used to being around older people, very difficult ones, I might add," she said with an inward impish smile, thinking of her uncle.

To her relief, Lord Darvey nodded. That was all the encouragement Elizabeth needed. "Given that I am applying for a position, I hope I may say without sounding immodest that I have a calm temperament, am not given to missishness, and am quite good at reading aloud." There. She did not know if she had said the right things, never having been a companion or even having met one, but she could not think of anything else that might sound like a proper qualification.

His Lordship turned up his hands in mock resignation. "What more is there to ask, especially since you come so well recommended by my colleague in the Royal Society? I think there's nothing for it but to offer you the job on behalf of my great aunt, who, by the way, is not difficult at all—a little different, perhaps, especially in her literary interests, but not difficult. I take it that you wish to accept?"

Mr. Eccleston rose to his feet from the leather chair that matched the one Elizabeth sat in. "Just a minute," he said, ignoring her vigorous assent. "I still have questions."

Lord Darvey, already having begun discussing wages and days off with Elizabeth, ignored him. Mr. Eccleston was reduced to shifting about impatiently, waiting for an opportunity to intervene.

He did not get it, however. Before he could engage her attention, Elizabeth, bird cage in hand, went away with Mrs. Mowbry, the housekeeper, to settle into the apartment next to that of her mistress and await that lady's eventual waking-up.

"I cannot believe you hired her just like that," the blond-haired man said pettishly when his Lordship was finally ready to listen to him. "Being incautious is totally unlike you, Justin. You don't know enough about her."

"Of course, I do." Lord Darvey looked down his arrogant, aristocratic nose at his shorter friend. "As I told you before she came, I had full particulars and assurances from Cranley. She is an orphan from a good family made penniless by a father who gambled. Cranley said the father was much older than the mother, though apparently the mother died about the same time. In any case, probably it was the father she was referring to when she said she's used to difficult older people."

"She's to be pitied, I'm sure," said Mr. Eccleston, sounding remarkably unsympathetic. "Still, I can't see why she isn't a governess or a companion to a young woman like herself. It doesn't seem natural for her to be willing to be cooped up with an old lady—even a nice one like Lady Treadway," he added hastily.

Lord Darvey grinned. "You're forgetting that Betsy doesn't mind," he said, referring to his great aunt's youthful maid. "Besides, if you were a young woman, would you take someone who looks like Miss Hanley into your employ?"

"That's my point. She's so. . . . She's very. . . ."

"Right. Fortunately, that does not interest me. I'm too involved with my work to pay attention to that sort of thing." Ignoring his friend's disbelieving look, he added, "Anyone as insouciant about my specimens as Miss Hanley appears to be is the proper person to be here. You know what a deuce of a time I've had trying to get staff. One glance at this room and the applicants are convinced that I'm a witch doctor or an ax-murderer. In any case, they don't want to stay here. She does want to, so that's good enough for me."

"Make light of what I'm saying if you like," Mr. Eccleston answered reproachfully, "but I know what I'm talking about. A companion is more a trusted member of the family than a servant, so if the position isn't filled by the right person, all sorts of havoc can occur. Why, we had an experience in my own family where the woman hired as companion to my cousin ran off with her husband's valet— and all of the silver." He reflected for a second, then added, "It was hard to tell whether they regretted the loss of the valet or the silver more."

His Lordship waved one hand in a gesture of dismissal. "The important thing is that I won't need to worry about her refusing to accompany my great aunt to my laboratory should Lady Treadway ever want to leave her room and visit me here, or resigning the first chance she gets because she disapproves of what I do. Never mind the rest. It doesn't matter."

With a supple grace unexpected in one so tall, Lord Darvey walked over to a specimen that reposed in isolated splendor on his worktable. Lifting it, he rubbed his open palm upon its naked dome, a gesture which would have gone far to confirm Elizabeth's worst fears if she'd seen it. "Let's not waste any more time talking about the help, Eccleston. Tell me how you've been progressing in your studies."

Mr. Eccleston was as devoted to geometry as his Lordship was to measuring skulls and therefore should have been delighted with the opportunity to expound upon his favorite topic. Apparently, however, he was not quite ready to give way on the subject of his friend's newest retainer.

Stretching out his legs in their too-large yellow breeches, he placed his badly polished boots upon the chair Elizabeth had vacated. "It doesn't make sense, Justin," he said, looking up at Lord Darvey with artless blue eyes. "Here you are, the most careful and logical of men, and yet you hire a woman about whom you know very little—and who looks more like a *chere amie* than a companion—without your giving it a thought. I know," he rushed on when Darvey started to interrupt, "she doesn't mind skulls. Still, that's hardly the test of a perfect companion, whatever you say."

"She's not a *chere amie*." To Mr. Eccleston's surprise, Lord Darvey's voice had a hard edge to it. "Not mine and not yours. She's what she says she is, pure and simple. And she's the one I mean for my great aunt to have for the position. What?" he queried as his friend began to mutter. "I can't hear you, Peter."

Mr. Eccleston pulled one of his green coattails forward and began to twist it. "All I said was that she may be pure, but I doubt that anything will be simple when there's a woman in residence who looks like Miss Hanley."

Lord Darvey let out an exasperated sigh. "Of course it will. I always have things simple; that's the way I like them."

He glanced with pleasure around his laboratory, which was simplicity itself. Besides the leather chairs, there were a large, highly polished ebony desk with a silver standish upon it, the worktable, and a number of mahogany shelves and cabinets for storage. There was very little else. No draperies covered the French windows leading out to neat, symmetrical flowerbeds in the neoclassical style, nor was there anything in the room that could even remotely be considered an ornament. The place was as controlled and well-ordered, as lean and masculine, as its owner.

In truth, the only disorderly element in it was the carelessly attired Mr. Eccleston.

"I suppose it will be all right if you say so. Still," Mr. Eccleston couldn't help adding, "I think in a year or two you should begin to consider acquiring a wife. If you had one, she'd be sure to find you all the staff you need and to keep everything going as it ought. Then you'd be altogether free to pursue your work. Well, what do you say?" He bowed his blond head slightly as though better to withstand the set-down certain to follow.

His Lordship yawned. "You may be right," he answered with Olympian indifference. "In fact, I've rather decided to see to it as soon as I have the opportunity."

"I said *a year or two*," Mr. Eccleston cried, "not soon." Instead of being pleased that Lord Darvey appeared ready to put his idea into action, his friend seemed quite dismayed. "Say you didn't mean it. You're still too young."

Lord Darvey laughed. "As young as you."

"That's what I said. Too young. In any case," Mr. Eccleston rallied his spirits, "this is not the sort of thing one does overnight. It takes thought and time and looking about among one's intimates and acquaintances for someone who might be appropriate. I know you haven't been engaged in doing any of those. Why, it could take months, years even, before you find the right woman." This thought so cheered him that he fell back in his chair beaming with delight.

His Lordship went over to his desk and extracted several sheets of paper from one of its cubbyholes. "It shouldn't take long at all," he replied, neatly slicing the air with the papers. "I've already done the preliminary part." When Mr. Eccleston only looked at him open-mouthed and did not speak, Lord Darvey pulled out one of the sheets and said, "I have here a list of reasons for and against matrimony. There are six, I think—yes, six—reasons in each column. For example, a reason against matrimony would be an increase of noise in the house. A reason for it is begetting an heir. It's all very straightforward. Do you have any questions so far?"

"Well, of course, I have." Peter Eccleston's good-natured face displayed a measure of disdain. "If you have six reasons for and six against, then you've reached a stalemate and can't do anything. I'm surprised you did not see that."

Lord Darvey grinned. "*But*, since I gave weights to items—increased noise earning a minus one, an heir earning plus five—matrimony came out a clear winner."

"You didn't tell me that." Mr. Eccleston looked aggrieved. "How was I to know? At any rate, putting things down on paper and finding a wife are vastly different, you must agree. For example, do you know what sort of wife you want? And where are you going to get her? Don't tell me you plan to spend your evenings at Almack's and at ton balls doing the pretty or give up Gentleman Jackson's to take some simpering miss for a ride in the park." This last was said with as much despair as though his old school chum had announced his intention to immolate himself.

His Lordship's long legs, encased in biscuit pantaloons that revealed the taut muscles beneath, bore him in a few strides to Mr. Eccleston's side. "It's in here." He thrust forward his lists. "I've worked it out so that nothing can go wrong."

"That's probably what Napoleon said to his generals before the Battle of Waterloo," his friend observed gloomily.

Lord Darvey removed Mr. Eccleston's legs from the other chair and reseated himself. "I'm not Napoleon," he rebutted scornfully. "I'm a natural philosopher. Now listen to what I've put down as being needful in a wife. First of all, she should not be ugly; that's for the sake of the children, so that they won't be, either. Second, she should not be too stupid; again, that's for the children. Third, she should not have a volatile disposition, so that there will always be a peaceful atmosphere; that will be good for us all. Last . . . and this is the most important item, I'm certain you'll agree . . . she should not want to stay about the house very much. What I mean is, she'll have to be the sort who has interests, charities, whatever those things are that females do to fill up their days, that will keep her from home and away from my laboratory. Well, what do you think?"

"I've never heard of anything so queer." Mr. Eccleston took hold of Lord Darvey's paper as gingerly as if it were a dead pet he did not want but could not quite bring himself to dispose of. Hurriedly he scanned it. "Everything you've got here is a negative . . . she should not this and she should not that. There isn't a single *should* in the lot. I don't think your approach is right. For all your obvious assets, I truly doubt that you'll find anyone suitable."

A lazy grin lightened his Lordship's handsome face. "Oh, I think I will. But if I don't, you, at least, will be pleased."

"I think I'd be pleased if you'd been this rigorous about Lady Treadway's companion. She seems a bit clumsy, you know, tripping over her bird cage the way she did."

"Why should I worry?" Lord Darvey said with uncharacteristic flippancy. "I have no intention of dancing with her." He tipped his dark head to stare up at the painted white ceiling. "I wonder how she's getting on."

In fact, at that moment Elizabeth was examining her pretty quarters and feeling she was getting on quite well. The apartment consisted of a large sleeping room dominated by a walnut bed whose four posts were hung with blue, white, and yellow crewelwork curtains. There were also several chairs with tables placed conveniently nearby, a dresser, and a very large wardrobe. Indeed, after stowing away the contents of her portmanteau, Elizabeth was hard put to fill even a corner of the wardrobe's cavernous interior.

To the left of the bedroom was a cozy sitting room, painted a cheerful yellow that matched the yellow in the bed curtains. It contained a blue and white settee and two padded wing chairs. She'd had nothing so nice in Lord Beowulf's house.

To her right was Lady Treadway's room. Dare she peak at her new employer? Unable to resist, Elizabeth opened the connecting door a crack and looked inside.

Lady Treadway's room was so stuffed with heavy, old-fashioned furniture that Elizabeth was unable to locate the person she knew must be within. Overcome by curiosity, she stuck her curly head a little farther into the room.

"Come in, do," a booming voice assailed her. "I don't

bite. Couldn't if I wanted to; I don't have my teeth anymore."

Trying not to giggle, Elizabeth pushed the door open all the way and entered the room. She was assailed immediately by the overpowering heat coming from the roaring fires in the two delft-tiled fireplaces. Used to the arctic cold of her uncle's house, Elizabeth was nearly overcome.

"Ah, a pretty one," the booming voice came again. "That's nice. We need good-looking people here to balance all those skulls." The voice abruptly stopped.

At least she had located Lady Treadway, Elizabeth thought. She was the little lump under the feather quilts in the vast Jacobean bed.

Elizabeth curtsied. "I am Elizabeth Hanley, your Ladyship. I am your new companion."

"I'm glad you're new," Lady Treadway cackled. "The old one died."

Elizabeth was unable to think of what to say to this remark, so she smiled and curtsied again. That must have been an acceptable thing to do, for she was then given permission to sit.

By the time Elizabeth dragged the heavy walnut chair up to the bed, Lady Treadway had emerged from beneath the covers, or at least enough of her had so that Elizabeth could see her face. It was a small, wizened face, rather like a dried apple, and it was covered by thin white hair under a white wool cap. "Like what you see?" Lady Treadway asked in a loud voice.

Elizabeth gave her a wide, dimpled smile, for indeed she did.

Lady Treadway returned the smile, thereby offering evidence that she had not exaggerated her lack of teeth. "Do you think we will get along? I can be demanding, you know."

"I'm certain we'll deal well together, my lady, although I would not mind hearing what you might demand."

Elizabeth's remark seemed to confuse the old woman.

"How do I know?" she finally muttered in a low voice that would have been loud for anyone else. "I'm a hey-go-mad person. It's one thing today and another tomorrow. I do like peppermints, however. And a glass of wine sometimes, especially when it's cold." Stopping her recitation, she jerked at the topmost cover to bring it farther up onto her tiny shoulders. "And books about naughty minxes. Have you ever read *Venus in Her Cloister, or the Nun in Her Smock?*"

So that was what his Lordship had meant about Lady Treadway's literary interests. "I'm afraid I haven't," she said, blushing rosily. She hoped her Ladyship didn't expect her to read such things aloud.

"Mustn't suppose I'm a blue stocking, though," Lady Treadway advised unnecessarily. "I used to live to dance."

"Is that so? I suppose you attended many balls and assemblies. Lady Treadway? . . . Lady Treadway?"

When Lady Treadway did not answer, Elizabeth put her fresh young face close to her employer's to make certain that the old woman was still breathing. She was, but she also was asleep.

Elizabeth got up quietly from her chair and started to walk to her own room. "*Memoirs and Adventures of a Flea,*" murmured her Ladyship. "That's another good one." Then she subsided once more.

Back in her own room, Elizabeth reviewed her conversation with Lady Treadway. Could her employer really expect her to read books with titles such as she had mentioned? It was going to be an interesting four months, she thought. She imagined herself sending her uncle lurid passages from *Venus in Her Cloister* instead of reports on Lord Darvey's researches, and she started to laugh.

She sobered quickly, however, for the plain truth was that she had been sent to be a spy, and as distasteful as that was, she had better not forget it. Her uncle wouldn't have been in the least amused by her fancies.

Once more she peeked into Lady Treadway's room to

affirm that the old lady was still sleeping. Seeing that she was, Elizabeth decided to return to his Lordship's laboratory. Although it was unlikely that she would learn anything of value on her first day there, she might as well begin as she meant to go on, she thought with a sigh.

To her relief, the room was unoccupied. Even though she'd been prepared to present his Lordship with an excuse for her presence, she was pleased that she did not need to—and delighted that it was unnecessary for her to face the not altogether friendly Mr. Eccleston.

Once again, she found herself impressed by the spartan neatness that marked the laboratory. She wondered if his Lordship's thinking was as orderly. If it were, then, indeed, he was a very different man from her uncle, whose logic, or lack thereof, often left her feeling helpless, if not angry—especially when he made absurd pronouncements on her sex.

How many times had he told her that, along with children and animals, women had small brains and thus were lacking in intelligence, every one? He gave her as "proof" for his thesis that when compared to men, women had small skulls.

The last time she'd been forced to listen to his theory was at the dinner table not so very long before he'd enmeshed her in his scheme against Lord Darvey. For some reason, she'd been particularly irked by it that night and had argued with him. "I could name two or three women in the neighborhood who have larger heads than their husbands," she'd said with a cool, little smile. "Therefore, I cannot see how you can be certain that their husbands must be more intelligent than they."

"Aha," said her uncle, brandishing his spoon at her. "You've proved my point! If you were more intelligent, you would be able to see it."

Elizabeth remembered how her hands had itched to empty the soup tureen over him. She had thrown them up in defeat, instead. Unconsciously she now repeated the gesture.

"What is it?" asked Lord Darvey, who'd come into the room without her being aware of it. "From the look of you, I'd say you are getting set to decamp already. I hope that isn't true."

Flushing, Elizabeth glanced up at him. How handsome he was, she thought with as much wonder as though she were seeing him for the first time. With his thick, dark hair and strong-boned face, he was as good to look at as the most attractive dandy ever to grace an assembly room. But despite his superior looks and fine clothes, obviously the handiwork of a master tailor, he wasn't a dandy; he was a natural philosopher, just like her uncle.

And she was a spy.

"That's the farthest thing from my mind," she answered truthfully, gazing into his long-lashed grey eyes. "If you are referring to my gesture, that was due to my feeling impressed by what I see. Everything appears to be so very well run."

Lord Darvey laughed. "I'd hardly say so. Do you know that I have to dust my laboratory myself because all the maids refuse to come in here, even our little Betsy who is otherwise fearless?"

"No, you don't mean it!" Elizabeth was obliged to laugh as well. "I cannot imagine you—that is, you do not seem . . ." Completely tangled in *cannots* and *do nots* which all seemed to lead to an expression of opinion that his Lordship appeared far too undomesticated even to know what a feather duster looked like, she gave it up. "If you wish, and Lady Treadway does not mind, I can take over that job for you," she said. "I could do it while she naps."

"Would you really?" Lord Darvey gave her an assessing look. "You know you would have to get near my specimens, perhaps even handle them." When Elizabeth nodded agreeably, he said in a warmly approving voice, "You're a right 'un. Old Cranley spoke the truth when he told me you'd be perfect for the post. I'll send off a note today thanking him."

Instead of acting gratified, Elizabeth blushed to the roots of her hair. She wasn't by nature devious and had made her offer spontaneously. She hadn't thought how it might aid her in gathering information. Still, the result would be the same. That made it difficult for her to accept his Lordship's well-meant praise.

"Why don't I show you about the place now?" Lord Darvey asked briskly in a gallant effort, it seemed to her, to ease what he took to be her shyness.

"Yes, please." She bobbed her head, causing her auburn curls to catch the light and shine with vibrant color.

His Lordship looked down thoughtfully at her. What was he thinking? Whatever it might have been, what he said was, "I probably should explain what I do here. I wouldn't want you to believe I'm into any skulduggery." Having delivered this dreadful pun, he gave her a slyly self-deprecating smile.

Elizabeth giggled, then said with as much mischievous intent as he'd put into his pun, "You'd be surprised by how interested I am, my lord. In fact, I'd like to know everything."

"Would you? Well, then, I shall take you at your word." His long fingers firm on her arm, Lord Darvey turned Elizabeth toward a set of shelves which covered a whole wall. "Why don't we begin here," he said, after first giving her a searching look. If his examination was to detect fear or faintness, her disclaimers of squeamishness to the contrary, there was surely no evidence of either; Elizabeth was too used to the sort of thing she was seeing. If anything, it was the touch of his hand on her arm which affected her sensibility, not his collection.

How very unlike her uncle he was, she thought once more after listening to his explanation of the physical differences among various races. Instead of behaving as though she were a dunderhead, incapable of more than the meanest understanding, he was treating her with a serious regard. She felt sure that no visiting natural philosopher could have been afforded a more thorough tour of his Lordship's laboratory.

"And now I think it is time to interrupt this lecture for some tea," his Lordship said. "I don't know what condition you are in, but my effusiveness has made me thirsty." Without stopping for her answer, he went to the door and ordered the waiting footman to fetch the tea tray.

"Will you pour for us, please?" he asked when it had come. "And while you do so, I shall be happy to answer any other questions you may have." He looked at her expectantly. "You do have some, don't you?"

In fact, Elizabeth had wondered about several things during the time she had been with him. When he had walked to the door to talk to the footman, for example, she had wondered whether his broad shoulders and narrow waist owed anything to his tailor's skill or were entirely the product of nature's beneficence. Trying to imagine his expression if she asked him that, Elizabeth blushed a brilliant red.

"No, no," he laughed, misinterpreting her response. "Do not be embarrassed. Fire away."

Desperately, she looked toward the ceiling, praying for inspiration. There must be something acceptable that she could ask. "Well, yes, I do have a question. My question is . . . ah . . . are you the only person in England who studies what you do?"

It was, of course, a ridiculous question because she of all people knew the answer to it; but there was no help for it.

"Indeed, I am not. There is at least one other, a foolish old excuse for a natural philosopher by the name of Beowulf. Like me, he is a Fellow of the Royal Society; otherwise, we are, I hope, nothing alike."

Elizabeth glanced quickly at his face and then down at her hands. "Is that so?" she mumbled.

His Lordship nodded. "And do you know why? The reason is that whereas I try to keep my personal prejudices separate from what I study, he only studies what he thinks will confirm his prejudices. I'm sure you'll agree that is hardly the mark of the unbiased student of nature."

"Oh, hardly." How well she knew that it was true.

Lord Darvey uncrossed his long legs to plant his beautifully polished boots firmly on the gleaming wooden floor. "The trouble is," he went on earnestly, "that because he preaches that the English male is superior in intellect to all others, which is, naturally, a very popular theory here, no one ever challenges him. It would be wonderful to have the evidence for such a conclusion, but I am not convinced that he has any."

Putting down his tea cup, he stood up restlessly and walked over to stand next to her. "Wouldn't you think that the members of the Royal Society, who certainly ought to know better, would at least question some of his wilder pronouncements?"

"I don't know," muttered Elizabeth, who was entertaining the idea that perhaps she also should have known better before embarking on her present course. "I mean, indeed yes." Trying to evade his icy gaze, which made her nervous even though she was aware she wasn't its real object, she rose to her feet as well.

His Lordship looked down into her troubled green eyes, and his stern expression softened. "I'm sorry," he said, laughing. "I shouldn't be going off like this in front of you. You don't know the culprit or are ever likely to, and I am sure that you could not care less about the subject. Besides, you must be tired."

His large hands grasped her shoulders and turned her toward the door. "I don't want you to do anything else today except go to your room and rest. Betsy can entertain Lady Treadway. If she asks, I'll explain to my great aunt that you could use a little peace before you officially take up your duties." Without waiting for her yea or nay, he steered her into the hall. "And I'll see you in here tomorrow with your duster, Miss Hanley."

Elizabeth sighed as she walked toward the stairs. How

was she to have peace when Lord Darvey not only refused to be impossible like her uncle but actually insisted upon being kind and thoughtful? Not to mention being so very handsome that a woman could easily forget what she had come for!

Three

"WELL, HAVE YOU done it?" Peter Eccleston demanded in funereal accents.

"Done what?"

Mr. Eccleston snorted inelegantly. "Don't play the fool with me, Darvey. You know very well what I mean. Have you thought about with whom you might want to enter Parson's Mousetrap?"

"My dear fellow. . . ." Lord Darvey smiled self-mockingly, then flipped up the tails of his blue morning coat so that he could comfortably seat himself in his favorite leather chair. "That sort of thing takes a little time even for someone as organized as I."

Mr. Eccleston flipped up his own tails, although his coat was already so wrinkled that it could hardly have mattered if he'd rolled in it upon the floor. Seating himself in the companion chair to his friend's, he proceeded to sneer, a gesture which seemed peculiarly inappropriate to his baby-ish, blue-eyed face. "Oh, really? I'm amazed that you haven't already made an exhaustive list of all the eligibles."

"I'll have it tomorrow. No, really, Eccleston, I am serious about what I told you, and I plan to do something about it rather soon. You mustn't be shocked or distressed, then, when I do."

Mr. Eccleston looked hurt, although he tried valiantly to

hide it. "Why should I care if you want to be foolish? And don't think it matters to me that we won't be able to be friends anymore, even though we've known each other since Eton."

"There you are." Lord Darvey uncrossed his booted legs and rose to put his hand upon Mr. Eccleston's shoulder. "I feared you were thinking something of the sort. I've told you what I want in a wife, someone who won't get in the way of my researches or of my friendship with you, either. You needn't worry that a woman will come between us and damage our association, Peter. I won't let that happen."

Obviously embarrassed, Mr. Eccleston wriggled away from his Lordship's reassuring hand. "I'm not really worried," he said pensively. "I just wouldn't want you to make a dreadful mistake."

Lord Darvey laughed, showing his gleaming white teeth. "I won't. I'm dealing with this problem as I would with one I'd face as a natural philosopher. Believe me, all will go as I mean for it to."

Seeing that he could not shake his Lordship's confidence in what he meant to do, Mr. Eccleston decided not to refer to the matter again, at least not for the next five or ten minutes. "How is the pretty companion getting on?" he asked. "Have you seen her since you hired her for your great aunt?"

Lord Darvey shifted a bit in his seat, and his breathing subtly altered. Peter Eccleston stared at him, his blue eyes narrowing with suspicion.

"Yes, I saw her," his Lordship said with an exaggerated lack of enthusiasm. "She came back to the laboratory yesterday afternoon." He followed this declaration with a yawn.

"You ought to get more sleep, old fellow. Why did she do that?"

Now that he thought about it, Lord Darvey had no idea why Miss Hanley had returned unbidden. He'd forgotten to ask. "She needed to know something from me about one of her duties," he lied so as to forestall the inevitable questions. "In any case, her presence was fortuitous. It gave me time to show her about the laboratory and to elicit a promise to dust it. Nobody else will."

"I can't believe it." Mr. Eccleston pulled himself from the large black leather chair and began to pace about in unshined Hessians, one of which was missing its tassel. "Did you actually give Miss Hanley a tour of this place?"

Looking rather annoyed, Lord Darvey nodded.

"But why?"

"What do you mean, why? I did it because she was here . . . and because she seemed interested in my work. She asked good questions." His Lordship's face was beginning to take on the aspect of a pagan god less than satisfied with a burnt offering. Apparently, he was not best pleased by his friend's queries or by the incredulous air with which they were offered.

Mr. Eccleston reseated himself, this time forgetting to first move his coattails aside. "I thought you specifically did not want a wife who would hang about your workroom. Why, then, would you want Lady Treadway's companion to do so? It's the same sex, you know," he remarked judiciously.

Lord Darvey's countenance displayed a slight flush. His voice, however, perhaps not without some effort of will, remained calm. "But it isn't the same situation. I don't plan to marry Miss Hanley, and if she becomes a nuisance, I'll get rid of her. I'll pass her on to you."

"I don't need a companion, Darvey; you're not thinking. Besides, don't tell me that you'd get rid of her. I happen to know that you're supporting every superannuated retainer your parents ever hired." Brow furrowed, Mr. Eccleston thought deeply for a moment, uninterrupted by his Lordship, who contented himself by scowling. "Why don't you?" he asked at last.

"Why don't I what?"

Mr. Eccleston fished behind him and pulled out a

handkerchief which he proceeded to tie into knots. "If you still insist on marrying, why don't you marry her? No, listen for a minute. Didn't you tell me Cranley said she comes from a good family fallen upon hard times?" Lord Darvey nodded. "Well, then, she's someone you might have met in town if she weren't down on her luck.

"On the other hand," he continued, obviously warming to his subject, "she has the advantage of being a servant more or less. What I mean is that if you told her to stay away from the house and not bother us, having been a servant she'd be submissive and do as you bid. Last, but by no means least, she is a remarkably attractive woman. Did you notice her . . . ?"

"That's enough." Lord Darvey put paid to his friend's commentary by knocking a tall container filled with shot against the edge of his worktable. "I shall choose someone—someone appropriate according to the list you saw—within the next week or two." He raised a large hand, still brown from his years of traveling in southern climes, to stop the explosion of words preparing themselves in Mr. Eccleston's mouth. "Actually, although I did not mention this to you previously, I've already more or less selected the woman I want. Now, all I have to do is ask her."

A teasing look came over his face. "No, no matter how you beg, I shall not tell you, Eccleston. First, I shall ask; then, if she says yes, I shall tell you. In fact, except for her family, you will be the first to hear."

"Oh, does she have a family? Are they anyone I know?" Mr. Eccleston widened his blue eyes and turned his mouth up in a boyish, innocent smile.

Lord Darvey put back his head and laughed. "It won't do, Eccleston. I shall not tell you aforehand. Why, suppose the cruel fair one refuses my offer?"

"Do you really think she might?" Mr. Eccleston looked with renewed optimism at his friend. His Lordship's response was a shrug of his well-tailored shoulders. For the present, Eccleston would have to content himself with that.

Standing up, Mr. Eccleston looked around for the papers he'd brought to show Lord Darvey, then walked away with them. "I'll be in the library if you want me," he advised, opening the connecting door to that room. "I still have a great deal to do on this problem." Waving one hand in farewell, he exited.

Lord Darvey frowned so hard that two long lines creased his wide forehead. Sometimes he wished Eccleston would not become so lonely working at home that he could not bear to stay there and must descend upon Grosvenor Square. It was no wonder that he, himself, wanted a wife who would be certain to absent herself. Including Lady Treadway, he already had as much company as he could tolerate.

He hadn't minded having Miss Hanley in his laboratory, however. In spite of her provocative face and lush body, there was something about her—what was it? She didn't seem coy and flirtatious like most women he'd met. Even the little maid Betsy and Mrs. Mowbry were prone to act that way with him, especially when they wanted something. In some ways, with her direct air, his great aunt's companion reminded him of a man.

Recalling her high breasts and the curve of her tiny waist from which even her plain, serviceable dress could not detract, he started to laugh. Still, it was true. He wondered if she had brothers who'd helped to raise her.

He shook his head, feeling irritated with himself. What did it matter who her relatives were? He had his experiments to do and no time to waste on foolish, idle thoughts.

Coincidentally, the unattractiveness of her wardrobe was in Elizabeth's thoughts then, too, perhaps because the garment she was wearing, even though refurbished with yellow ribbons, was such a grim reminder of her uncle's parsimony. Although she had returned to her room to add a lace apron to the old brown ruffed dress, it was still as tired looking as all the other times she'd worn it in the last two years. It was unfortunate, she thought, that she didn't have anything better looking to put on. Perhaps after she received her first quarter's wages, she'd buy some lengths of material and make herself two or three new gowns.

"Oh, Primrose," she said, turning a troubled face to her pet canary. "Is it very wrong to spend money on oneself obtained from a man on whom one is spying?"

The canary tilted his yellow head to one side, seeming to consider the moral conundrum with which he'd been presented. Then he hopped about feverishly and began to scold.

"Of course, you are right," said Elizabeth, sounding as cross as crabs. "You always are. But I do not wish to hear it just now." She showed him her back, and after a few minutes she left the room without having engaged her disobliging pet in further discourse.

Collecting an ostrich plume feather duster from one of the maids, she made her way downstairs to Lord Darvey's laboratory to dust his specimens as she'd promised she would do. And if she managed to discover something today, the reporting of which would do Lord Darvey no harm and David some good, well, that would be acceptable, she consoled herself.

It would be better, naturally, if his Lordship were not there; her feelings of guilt would be less if she did not have to look at him. As it transpired, however, when she opened the door and discovered him within, tall and elegantly turned out, she could not help but smile. Apparently, whether she would or not, it gave her pleasure to see him.

Expecting the invader to be Peter Eccleston, Lord Darvey responded to the opening of the door with a frown. Elizabeth's mouth tightened at the chilly welcome, causing her smile to waver.

When he saw who the intruder was, his Lordship's handsome, rather austere features relaxed. "Come in," he invited. "You will not be in the way." He pointed toward the cluster of feathers that Elizabeth clutched to her midriff.

"If you're planning to use that thing to dust, I'd be most grateful for it."

Quietly, so as not to disturb him in his work, Elizabeth walked to the rows of shelves closest to the hall door. There she set to with her duster.

The first objects to receive her ministrations were several large specimens, large enough that her uncle would undoubtedly have claimed them as members of his favorite race and sex. After them, she gently dusted a number of small skulls with prominent cheekbones. She thought they rather resembled each other. Perhaps they had once belonged to members of the same family. Although their original owners had very likely gone to their just rewards long, long before she'd come to his Lordship's house, Elizabeth felt saddened by her thought . . . and homesick once more for her brother. The stillness in the room was broken by her sigh.

"What is it?" His Lordship turned to her. "Does the sight of my specimens depress you? I must say I've been surprised at how easily you seemed to accept them."

Elizabeth's smile was rueful. "I was missing my brother," she told him candidly. "Skulls do not trouble me. I've been looking at them for years."

"I knew there had to be a brother," Lord Darvey announced triumphantly, following that with a hasty, "What did you say?" His dark eyebrows shot upward. "How is that, pray tell?"

She'd done it now. How, indeed?

Walking slowly to purchase a bit of time, Elizabeth made her way to the opposite wall. *Think*! she commanded herself, and, obediently, from some little crevice of her mind, her memory plucked a curious story her uncle had once related to her. Because she did not know what else to say, it would have to do.

"There was a hill near our house," she informed Lord Darvey, seating herself, at the beckoning wave of his hand, in the black chair opposite the one he took. Nervously, she smoothed out the wrinkles in her brown dress. "Well, it was not actually a hill but more a sort of mound. In any case, it contained human remains and many other interesting things, such as jewelry and swords and pieces of broken vases."

"Really?" Lord Darvey leaned forward in his chair, seeming, to her relieved surprise, to be quite taken with her tale.

Elizabeth's little pink tongue flicked out to moisten her dry lips. She gave him a tentative smile. "Yes, and my brother and I used to dig into the mound when no one else was about to see us, and we would find these things, including skulls, and smuggle them home."

"Is that so? And where are the skulls now?" Apparently, her references to the other objects did not interest him at all. "You still have them, don't you?"

A vision of a yawning pit flashed before Elizabeth's eyes. Once again, she was in dangerous territory. If she answered his Lordship's question in the affirmative, he'd likely insist upon setting off immediately to collect her finds. "Oh, no. Mama came upon our cache and disposed of it. Then, later," she tacked on quickly, in an effort to protect herself on all counts, "when we had to sell the property to pay Papa's debts, the new owner had the mound flattened so that he could build something upon it."

Lord Darvey's lips tightened. "Pity," he murmured. "Still, it's a fascinating story."

"Thank you." Modestly, Elizabeth lowered her long, thick lashes. She was rather pleased with it herself.

His Lordship scrutinized her countenance a space. Then he said, "Do you know that besides Eccleston, who has his own pursuits and cannot maintain an interest in anything he can't plot an orbit for, you are the only person here who isn't revolted by what I do. Tell me, if Lady Treadway can spare you sometimes, would you be willing to help me?"

"But, of course," Elizabeth answered readily, raising

herself from the chair. "Now where did I put that duster? Oh, good; here it is."

Lord Darvey stood up next to her and placed his right hand on her arm. "No, I mean really help me. You could be my assistant. It would not take me long to train you—and perhaps if you had something new to think about, you might not miss your brother quite so much." His fingers squeezed her arm in reassurance.

Elizabeth felt a frisson of pleasure course up from the spot he touched and come to rest somewhere in her middle. She told herself that it was caused by his kindness and her satisfaction with his offer.

Certainly her uncle Beowulf would never have permitted her to assist him if she remained in his household forever. Not that his rejection of her in this regard was a personal rejection. It simply was of a piece with his amazement that females managed to walk upright like men instead of going about on all fours like the other animals or swinging through the trees.

"Well, what do you think?"

"I'd be delighted." Elizabeth's pretty face shone with pleasure. "When shall I begin?"

Lord Darvey gave her a broad smile. "Why not now? You can help me measure the crania of this lot." He pointed to a group of skulls set out neatly on the big worktable.

"Measure crania!" Elizabeth's dimples flashed. "I've always wanted to do that."

Lord Darvey laughed. "Of course you have. So let me show you how to accomplish it without any more delay. It's simple, really. Watch me." He proceeded to pour lead shot into the cranium of a large, grinning skull until it was full. Then he measured the amount used by pouring it into a graded container. "The more of these I need, the larger the brain must have been," he concluded, noting the amount in a book. "Now, isn't that simple?"

He took down one of the small skulls Elizabeth had been dusting. "Let me show you how different two specimens can be," he announced eagerly, preparing to repeat the operation. "Oh, drat!"

Somehow, his Lordship had missed his mark. The consequence was that a shower of lead shot rolled onto the table and from there every which way on the floor.

"Let me help you, my lord." Elizabeth hitched up her skirts a little and got on her knees beside him. She scooped up a fistful of shot, then tilted her head to look into his smoke-colored eyes, now more nearly on a level with hers.

Time seemed to slow and get slower. "The beads," she said stupidly, swaying toward him and holding out the shot.

"Yes." Lord Darvey sounded distracted, and there was a thin film above his upper lip which had not been there before. "No . . . I mean no, they aren't beads. Please stand up, Miss Hanley. I shall do so as well."

"But the . . . uh . . . beads," she repeated, protesting. "Most of them are still there."

Lord Darvey put his arms about Elizabeth and began to lift her. "Never mind," he replied curtly. "I do not want them." Swiftly, he jerked her the rest of the way to her feet.

The sound of material separating caused the two of them to look down. "Oh, dear." She could not hide her dismay. "My dress is torn."

And so it was. The brown dress that she had worn for ages, and already turned once, was now fit only for the rag bag. There was a large rent in the skirt where Lord Darvey must have caught the material under his boot. "It does not matter," she said in a too-high voice, trying to sound cheerful. "I never liked it anyway."

"You should have new clothes." His Lordship looked provoked. "New and pretty ones, in attractive colors. I shall go this instant and get you money to purchase them. I always keep some funds in the library." Seeming to recollect something, he said, "I shan't go in there now. Tomorrow, I'll leave a purse for you."

Elizabeth stared at him, her mouth rounded and half-open in shocked surprise. What did he take her for, an object of charity? "No, you will not," she said decisively. "I will wait until I receive my salary."

"My dear Miss Hanley," Lord Darvey said, sounding like a schoolmaster faced with an impertinent pupil, "as much as I might admire your outspokenness and independence—and I do—I'm afraid they are not very suitable in a companion. In other words, I think you are going to have to let me be the judge for Lady Treadway of what your needs are and how they're to be met."

Uncharacteristically, Elizabeth could not think what to reply.

His Lordship's manner thawed a little. "All the staff gets a clothing allowance, you know—or perhaps you didn't know. It isn't charity; it's my custom. In your case, it's even more important that you accept it, for the sake of Lady Treadway's consequence. You can understand that, can't you?"

Although she knew nothing about what he did for the servants, she had the feeling that he had invented that last reason on the spot. Hadn't he told her just the day before that Lady Treadway rarely left her room? She started to refuse once more. Then she looked into his darkening grey eyes.

"Yes, my lord." Elizabeth bent her head till her slender neck showed white and vulnerable below her auburn curls.

"Good." Lord Darvey's voice noticeably gentled. "Oh, and one thing more. Take Betsy with you and one of the footmen. I do not want you to go out alone; you are too . . . Never mind; just do as I ask. Agreed?"

What could she say? Defeated, Elizabeth moved her slim shoulders in a gesture of compliance. "Thank you," she whispered. "You are very good."

Before she could say anything more, the door leading from the library was flung open and Peter Eccleston entered the room. "I need your help, Justin. Nothing I do makes this come out. Why, Miss Hanley. I didn't expect to find you here. Not that I'm not pleased, of course. What happened to your skirt?"

His Lordship looked coldly at his friend. "Blast it, Eccleston. Can't you ever knock?"

Oh, dear, thought Elizabeth, eyeing the untidy Mr. Eccleston. She did not want to be interrogated again. In fact, she did not want to be here at all. She wanted to return to her room in order to think about the events of the morning.

Now was probably her best opportunity to escape. Inclining her head, she curtsied to the men. "If you'll excuse me, my lord, Mr. Eccleston, I shall return upstairs to take up my duties." Before either gentleman could further engage her, she quickly walked away.

"What was she doing here this time?" Mr. Eccleston questioned. Then he spied the spilled shot and the discarded feather duster. "What happened here? It looks like . . ." His words stopped on a gasp. "Good heavens, Darvey, never tell me you ripped her skirt!"

His Lordship's reply was a fulminating look.

"My dear man, I'm sorry if I've offended; it's just that I'm so surprised. I've never thought of you as a molester of women, you see."

Lord Darvey gritted his perfect white teeth. "If you don't stop, Peter, I shall molest you. How many times do I have to tell you that I have no interest in Miss Hanley in any personal way? I had a little accident, is all, and she threw down her duster, with which she had been dusting, not cavorting or trifling with me, so that she could help me. Then I accidently stepped on her skirt. That is the whole of it." He hesitated. "I suppose, though, I'd better mention, in case you get any more peculiar ideas, that she will be assisting me here from now on. I suggest you get used to that fact—or find another place to work on your studies. And now, you must excuse me as well."

"Where are you going? Would you like me to accompany you?"

His Lordship lowered his dark brows and glowered. "I am going to your house. It is quieter there. And, no, you may not accompany me. Stay here."

Elizabeth awoke the next morning brimming with delighted anticipation. Nothing could dampen the feeling. Even if Lord Darvey's largess made it harder than ever for her to feel comfortable about spying on him, she could not but be thrilled at the thought of purchasing a new wardrobe.

By half after nine, however, when she'd still had no communication with him, she began to wonder if his Lordship had forgotten his offer. "Oh, well," she sighed, removing her old brown cloak again and hanging it on the outside of the large wardrobe, "perhaps it is better this way."

A few minutes later a footman knocked at her sitting room door. "This is from his Lordship," he said, turning over a plump purse. "And I've some messages for you, also." Rather pompously he cleared his throat. "His Lordship said not to forget you mustn't go out unattended. Mr. Hemmings told Betsy and Roger to be ready to leave with you. Oh, yes, and Mr. Eccleston wishes to see you in the laboratory."

Now what did he want, Elizabeth wondered unhappily. He probably had another thirty questions to ask her that he'd thought of during the night.

When she entered the laboratory, she found her employer's friend looking rather agitated. "Have you spoken with Lord Darvey this morning?" he asked before she had gotten very far into the room. "The butler tells me that he is away from home, and I thought you might know when he plans to return."

Elizabeth shook her head. "I have not seen him since yesterday. Did you have an appointment with him? I do not think it would be like him to forget."

Mr. Eccleston tugged hard at his already askew neckcloth. "An appointment? No. I just supposed he'd be here to help me with my problem. He is an excellent mathematician, you know, as well as a natural philosopher. Now I'm afraid I shall just have to stand about until he returns."

"I shall ask someone to bring you coffee." Elizabeth gave him a polite smile, then curtsied and made for the door. "If you will excuse me, two of the staff are waiting to accompany me on a shopping expedition. I'm to buy some new clothes."

"Really?" Mr. Eccleston's friendly look suggested he'd managed to get over his reservations about her. "I love to help people shop for clothes. Are you going to Oxford Street? I shall go with you."

Although she tried valiantly, Elizabeth was unable to dissuade him from joining her. Thus, a short time later she set off as part of an improbable combination of a companion-spy, a maid, a footman, and a badly dressed geometer.

To Elizabeth's surprise, Mr. Eccleston turned out to be an asset to their little group. Despite his rumpled look, his clothes were expensive, and every assistant in every shop they entered appeared to know it and put forth an extra effort to be helpful. In much less time than she had anticipated, Elizabeth was the entranced possessor of several dress lengths of muslin, wool, and twill as well as an assortment of hats, pelisses, and hose. To this booty, Mr. Eccleston insisted upon contributing some feathers and four bunches of artificial flowers.

"Now," said he, as, laden with packages, they stood on the pavement outside of Clark and Debenham's, "we must take some refreshment. Follow me."

"I do not think so, Eccleston," said a voice marked by irritation, and the group looked to the road to see a less than amiable Lord Darvey descend from his carriage.

Mr. Eccleston's free hand nervously went to his high-crowned beaver, which he managed to make even more skewed than it had been. "Why, Darvey," he croaked in the voice of a small boy caught with his fingers in the honey jar, "I didn't expect to see you here. What a coincidence."

His Lordship did not deign to answer but moved in a straight line for where they stood. "Oh." Elizabeth jumped back guiltily, although she was uncertain what she'd done. Could he have decided some time between yesterday and this morning that her mound story was so much gammon? Or, much, much worse, could he have learned somehow that she was a spy? No, whatever it was that irked him, she felt sure that in some way it involved Mr. Eccleston. She hoped Lord Darvey did not think she'd enticed his friend from his work.

His Lordship removed the several parcels Mr. Eccleston was juggling and presented them to the others. "You must go home, Miss Hanley," he ordered. "You are needed there. As are both of you." He looked down his nose at Roger and Betsy. "You may take Mr. Eccleston's carriage. You, Peter, will of course wish to accompany me." With that, he grasped Mr. Eccleston securely by the arm and led him off.

"What was the cause of that?" asked Betsy when the three had seated themselves in the carriage. "I never saw his Lordship act put out that way before." Slowly, Elizabeth shook her head. It was a puzzle to her.

Peter Eccleston was puzzled as well. It wasn't like Darvey to show his feelings so openly or even to have many feelings to show; except for a few things, such as the intellectual stupidity of certain people who should know better, he was a remarkably tolerant and even-tempered person.

What sin had he, Eccleston, committed to have caused his friend's disapproval? All he'd done was enjoy the company of Lady Treadway's lovely companion. He hadn't even lusted after her. Well, perhaps he had lusted a little. He smiled to himself, thinking of her high-breasted figure and shining green eyes. Then he looked up at his friend's grey, distant orbs and the provocative picture vanished. "My dear fellow," he protested, but Darvey raised his hand to stop him.

"Not now, Eccleston. Not until we're back in Grosvenor Square." Then he launched into a description of the skulls he'd bought that morning which he kept up until the two were seated in his laboratory.

"Well, Peter?" The men faced each other from the black chairs. "I'm waiting for you to tell me why you were with Miss Hanley. Was it necessary for you to accompany her to the shops?"

"Why, yes," Peter answered in a starchy tone. "You wouldn't want a lady to go about unescorted, would you?"

His Lordship stretched his long, booted legs in front of him. "In the first place, she is not a 'lady' in the conventional sense but a hired companion. And in the second place, as you couldn't have failed to notice, she already had an escort. Tell me, what were they occupying themselves with while you were doing their job?"

In truth, Peter could hardly recall their presence. "They helped in the shops," he said, flushing a bit. "How the devil do I know what they were doing?"

"Well, then, what were you and Miss Hanley doing?"

Mr. Eccleston looked indignant. "For heaven's sake, Justin, you should hear yourself. You sound like the Grand Inquisitor." When his friend ignored this statement and continued to wait like a stone for Mr. Eccleston's response, that gentleman answered hotly, "What do you think we were doing? She bought some things . . . I don't know, cloth and frippery things . . . and we talked about geometry."

"Ha," said his Lordship, raising his dark brows.

"Well, we did." Mr. Eccleston smiled with remembered satisfaction. "She is intelligent, and as you told me yourself, she asks good questions. I explained to her the theory of least squares and she was fascinated."

Justin fixed his friend with a cold, skewering look. "I won't have it, Eccleston. Both of us know there's but one reason why men of our station pay attention to women in Miss Hanley's position, and that is out of plain animal desire."

"Is that why you have enlisted her to assist you with your work?" Mr. Eccleston asked innocently.

Lord Darvey looked taken aback. Then his features hardened again. "Certainly not," he replied haughtily. "I wasn't talking about myself. If you will stop to remember, as I also told you when I referred to Miss Hanley's ability to ask good questions, she has no interest for me other than as a person who can help me in my laboratory, and entertain my great aunt, of course. I assure you, she has no other appeal."

So engrossed were they in their discussion that neither was aware that Elizabeth, come down to thank his Lordship for his generosity, was standing at the door. Nor were they aware that, her head and body held stiffly as though they might otherwise come apart, she walked swiftly away after hearing Lord Darvey's words.

"So, is it settled?" His Lordship looked at Mr. Eccleston, and at the other's nod, Lord Darvey visibly relaxed. "Well, then, it is time for you to wish me happy. Miss Brimmer has agreed to be my wife."

"Who?" asked Mr. Eccleston, sounding perplexed. "I've never heard of her."

Four

"OF COURSE, YOU'VE heard of her." His Lordship's expression was less than pleased. "In fact, you were introduced to her just last week. Don't you remember? She was standing outside with her mother and brother when I brought you over to meet them."

"Outside? Do you mean outside this house?" Mr. Eccleston grabbed at his wrinkled neckcloth as though it were about to throttle him. "Oh, no, you can't mean it; not that scraggy young thing with the fade-away voice."

As quick as a cat, Lord Darvey was out of his chair. "Go home, Eccleston," he ordered in a voice sheathed in ice. "And do not trouble yourself to come back."

"Upon my soul. You do mean it." Ignoring his friend's decree of banishment, Mr. Eccleston rose to give him a congratulatory thump upon the back. "My dear fellow, I couldn't be more delighted," he said heartily, without any apparent discomfort at his hypocrisy. "But, um, would you mind telling me your reasons for choosing her?"

His Lordship hesitated, undecided as to whether he should accept the proffered olive branch. Then he shrugged his broad shoulders in resignation. "I should think it would be obvious, Eccleston. She meets all four of my criteria, not excluding the one that she will rarely be about."

"I don't see that." Mr. Eccleston peered at him with

worried-looking blue eyes. "Are you certain? It seems to me, from what I remember of her, that she's just the sort who would want to cling to you."

Lord Darvey scooped up a quantity of lead shot from a canister and proceeded to shift it from one long-fingered hand to the other. "You only say that because you don't know her. If you had studied her, as I have done, you'd soon perceive that above everything she likes her mother and brother; they are very nearly her only interest. Thus, she will want to be with them instead of with me. And since they live in the very next house to this, well, nothing could be easier; she can trot over and spend every day there with them." A modest smile traced his lips as he awaited the approval his cleverness so obviously merited.

"If you say so." With an absent expression, Mr. Eccleston helped himself to some of his friend's lead shot. "But did you ever think that instead of Miss Brimmer wanting to spend her time next door with her family, they might want to come here and spend their time with her? Then there would be all those extra people underfoot instead of just one. I shouldn't imagine you'd care for that a great deal. I certainly wouldn't."

Lord Darvey frowned. "I must confess I hadn't conceived of the possibility. That would be the very devil. I'd never get anything accomplished then."

Returning the shot to its receptacle, his Lordship began to pace about the room, his hands clasped behind him. Within a short space, however, he returned to stand next to his friend. "The problem is solved," he asserted with his customary cool self-assurance. "I shall simply explain to Fidelia the necessity for a quiet atmosphere, which means that she and her clan will need to congregate someplace else. She will be reasonable about it, I assure you."

Peter Eccleston gave his friend a doubtful look. "You certainly put a deal of faith in reason, don't you, Darvey?"

"Well, of course I do. The world could not have advanced without it."

"Perhaps." Mr. Eccleston's fingers tapped at his mouth. "Still, I would not rule out trouble."

"Trouble? What sort of trouble?" His Lordship's dark brows drew down in a look that said he did not approve of trouble; trouble got in the way of one's researches.

Mr. Eccleston replaced his handful of shot, too; then he reseated himself in the black leather chair. "Not with your Miss Brimmer," he explained, shaking his blond head. "I agree with you that she's the sort that can easily be broken to harness. No, the one I'd be concerned about is her mother. I have a suspicion that she's the critical type."

"And what is that to me?" his Lordship said in a haughty voice. "Everything goes as I wish; there is nothing here to criticize."

"Ah, but if she's the way I think she is, she'll find something. Perhaps she'll want you to put more furniture and paintings in the rooms. Or maybe she'll feel that the staff needs smartening up. Or she might try to convince Lady Treadway to choose a companion more in the usual mold."

"I'd like to see . . . !" Lord Darvey stopped himself. "So it's the companion again, is it? Why are you always bringing up the companion, Eccleston? For the last time, let me tell you that she isn't especially important."

"If you say so," Mr. Eccleston said brightly. Then he muttered under his breath, "Care to wager that your mother-in-law won't agree?"

After hearing his Lordship pronounce her a creature of low and limited appeal, it would hardly have surprised Elizabeth to learn that he considered her insignificant as well. It would not have surprised her, but it would have made her more offended than she already was, which was quite offended, indeed.

"Animal desire, is it! If I hadn't promised Uncle I'd remain until after that silly lecture, we'd be on our way back to Epsom this minute," Elizabeth informed her canary in a wrathful tone. "How dare Lord Darvey think of me in that disgusting way!"

Truth to tell, when Elizabeth considered her place in the household it was not as a servitor but as a member of the upper classes acting (to her shame) as a spy and imposter. Thus, she found Lord Darvey's classification of her not only demeaning but also outrageous.

His profession of a lack of interest in her as a female distressed her, too, although she had no intention of ever revealing it to her confidant and could barely stand to think of it herself. The fact was that although she knew she should have been glad that his Lordship, at least, would never entertain lecherous thoughts about her, she wasn't. If anything, that part of his remarks bothered her more than the rest.

Flushing, Elizabeth said, "The dust could collect in *piles* on his Lordship's nasty skulls, and I would not care."

"Chirp," Primrose offered softly, for once sounding sympathetic.

Uncoiling from the blue and white sofa where she had flung herself, Elizabeth began to pace rapidly about her comfortable sitting room. "Do you know," she continued her address, "now that I'm aware of what a base, contemptible person Lord Darvey is, I am not the least bit sorry that I'm here to spy on him. As a matter of fact, I'm glad. He does not deserve any better."

She seated herself at a small French lady's desk set catercornered on the fireplace wall. "So be it," she intoned grimly. Taking a pen and paper from the standish, she dipped the pen into the ink pot and prepared to write to her uncle.

A cacophony of bird sounds caused Elizabeth to turn in her chair. "What is it, Primrose?" she asked impatiently. "Surely, you cannot object to my corresponding with my uncle? I am only telling him about Lord Darvey's system of organizing his specimens, which I had meant to do in any case."

As though responding to a plan to run off with the family plate, the canary let loose with another explosion of sound. "Stop that, you stupid bird," Elizabeth demanded indignantly. "You don't know anything about it." Throwing down her pen, she walked over to the cage and began tugging at its cover. "I don't need to listen to you," she announced defiantly.

A soft tap at the door caused Elizabeth to blush and drop her hand. "Come in," she called and stood without moving until she saw who was there.

"I'm sorry to interrupt, Miss." Lady Treadway's young maid, Betsy, curtsied and then looked around in puzzlement. "It's the funniest thing," she said, screwing up her little nose, "but I could have sworn I heard you fussing at someone. I couldn't have, though, could I? There's no one here."

"Indeed not," Elizabeth agreed readily, having no inclination to confess that she had arguments with a bird. "Have you come for something in particular, Betsy?"

"Goodness, I forgot for a minute." The girl clapped a hand to her blond, mob-capped head. "I have a message for you from his Lordship. He wants everyone to come to the inner hall. You and me is to escort her Ladyship."

"We are? Why would he want us all there?" When Betsy only looked blank, a noticeably paler Elizabeth said, "I wonder if it has anything to do with our going shopping with Mr. Eccleston. Do you think his Lordship means to scold us in front of everyone? I would dislike it excessively if he did."

"His Lordship would never do anything like that." Laughing, Betsy dismissed the suggestion out of hand. "He's too kind to do that." She ignored the unladylike snort with which Elizabeth punctuated the reference to Lord Darvey's benevolent nature. "Now, let's do something about your hair. If you don't mind me saying so, it looks like your canary's been running through it."

Reaching over, Elizabeth pushed back the flowered

material that half-covered Primrose's cage. "I'm sorry," she whispered. "I shouldn't have done that."

"I knew I heard you say something before." Betsy's blue eyes sparkled. "It was to the bird, wasn't it?" When Elizabeth nodded, Betsy said with a laugh, "At least I know I'm not barmy. Isn't it nice you have a friend to talk to who can't answer back?"

Elizabeth's laugh joined the maid's, although the expression on her pretty face seemed more rueful than amused. "We'd better get on with it," she prompted. "Whatever the reason, Lord Darvey is waiting for us."

By the time the three women arrived at the inner hall, most of the rest of the staff was already assembled there, even the coachmen and grooms who lived in the mews beyond. Elizabeth watched as the footmen put down her Ladyship's chair next to where Lord Darvey stood. Then she and Betsy arranged their mistress' slipping shawls and blankets. Immediately after, Elizabeth escaped to the back row, beside a marble column holding a bust of a thoughtful-looking Sir Isaac Newton.

Even if Lord Darvey did not mean to chastise her in front of the staff, she thought, she did not want to stand directly before him, to see him and be seen; her feelings were still too raw. Bending her knees, she sank until the only thing visible to her of Lord Darvey was the top of his thick, ebony hair.

His Lordship had been waiting for her. One could hardly be expected to make an important announcement without everyone in attendance, could one? But where the deuce was she now?

When he spotted her, *skulking* in the back row, he was overcome by a wave of irritation. He had anticipated having her directly before him. Wasn't it his right as the owner of this house to look at Miss Hanley when he wished?

Of course, even without seeing her, he could imagine her sweetly sensuous face with its halo of auburn curls. It was sharp in his mind, whereas when he attempted to recapture his fiancée's look he could get nothing at all no matter how he tried. Surely, there was proof, if any were needed, that it was better to wed and bed someone like Fidelia Brimmer, who would never distract a man from his real concerns, than a dasher like Miss Hanley.

"Get on with it, dear Justin," his great aunt said in her loud voice. "Some of us have other things to do."

Ignoring the muffled giggles, Lord Darvey said imperturbably, "I've had you brought together to give you the happy news that I am affianced to a young woman named Miss Fidelia Brimmer. Some of you will recognize the name immediately, for she happens also to be our neighbor in the house on the left."

He paused and waited for the ripple of excited comments to subside. "My fiancée and her mother and brother may want to visit from time to time in order to familiarize themselves with her future home and staff. In fact, they are expected to take tea here this afternoon." Rising slightly on his toes to get a better view of the crouching Miss Hanley, he added, "I know you will be ready to offer them every assistance and welcome them with courtesy and good will." He moved back a little from his position and ended his announcement with a smile.

"Congratulations," said Lady Treadway loudly, her smile adding more wrinkles to her small, lined face. "It's past time for you to fill the nursery, I'm sure we all agree. When is the wedding to be?"

Lord Darvey laughed. "Do not worry. We shall be certain to make it for when you aren't otherwise engaged, Great Aunt. Actually. . . ." He sounded much less definitive now. "We have not chosen a date yet. Some time next year, I think. I promise to let all of you know far enough in advance for you to arrange your calendars."

He accompanied his last remark with a teasing grin, but his present mood did not match it. As he'd spoken, he had realized that he was in no hurry to get leg-shackled to his fiancée. Let it suffice for now that he'd taken the first step, he thought. There was no need to rush the rest.

He accepted the congratulations that Hemmings, the butler, offered in the name of the entire staff. Then he watched as the servants went scurrying to make certain everything was perfect for the visit of their future mistress and her family.

When Elizabeth tried to make good her escape with the others, however, Lord Darvey would not let her. With quick steps he strode to her side and grabbed her small, delicate wrist. "Do not go away," he said. "I wish you to attend me in the library to receive my instructions about my great aunt."

Although she did not understand the why of it, Elizabeth had felt angrier than ever since his announcement. It was too bad that she could not refuse to go with him. Begrudging every movement, she shuffled along in his wake until they reached the book-lined room. Then she trailed him past long, polished tables laden with neat stacks of publications to a grouping of Adam chairs and sofas covered in soft blue velvet and seated herself without waiting for permission.

As Lord Darvey turned to face her, she could not help but think what a very handsome man he was; she had to give him that. With his black hair arranged in a windswept and his strong, patrician features, he was masculine perfection. His figure, immaculately clothed in a snugly fitting blue coat of superfine and fawn breeches, was top of the trees as well.

Good looks weren't everything, however. "You wished to see me, my lord?" she asked starchily.

Apparently, his Lordship was not much in charity with her, either. "That is why I asked you to accompany me, Miss Hanley, that is, if you do not mind."

"How could I mind, my lord? I am here to serve."

Her words were proper enough, but there was an acid edge to Elizabeth's voice which made Lord Darvey look curiously at her. Unfortunately, because she refused to lift her head, he could not read the expression in her lovely green eyes; she was thwarting him again.

"Is something wrong, Miss Hanley? You seem rather . . . dissatisfied."

"I? How could I be, my lord? It is not for me to be anything other than satisfied." She accompanied this patently insincere statement with the smile of one sucking a lemon.

Lord Darvey's black brows suddenly went up. "Good heavens. It's the shopping expedition. That's why you're so thin-skinned now, isn't it?"

He was getting close to the truth. "I do not know what you mean," she stuttered as her face turned pink.

"I mean that you are still upset because I insisted that you purchase new clothes. Confess. I've guessed it, haven't I?"

Elizabeth looked stricken. Her new clothes! In her bitterness over his belittling remarks, she had forgotten about the dress materials she had purchased at his expense, forgotten how generous and thoughtful he had been. For the first time since her parents' death she would have a pretty wardrobe, and it was due entirely to this man. It should not matter what he said about her.

Well, perhaps that was doing it too brown; but he had not spoken for her ears, and it was not his fault that she had overheard him. What must be remembered was that in his treatment of her, his Lordship had been more than kind, certainly more than she deserved considering why she was there.

Elizabeth lifted her beguiling face to Lord Darvey, who was still waiting for her reply. "No, of course I am not upset," she said with such gravity that he could not help but smile. "In fact, I am very grateful and must beg your pardon for not having thanked you before."

His Lordship's right hand sketched a quick, dismissive gesture, but Elizabeth could tell that he was pleased. All he said, however, was, "Have Betsy help you with your sewing. I want to see the results soon."

"Yes, my lord." Elizabeth self-consciously smoothed her old figured green muslin, then dimpled up at him. "But now, won't you tell me why you asked me here? Surely, it could not have been to discuss my clothes. What may I do for you?"

For a second, Lord Darvey's grey eyes gleamed. Then, barely perceptibly, he shook his head. "What I wanted was to ask you to try to curb my great aunt's tongue when she meets the future new additions to the family later; outflank her, as it were. I recognize that I'm asking a great deal, but I think you realize that the effort needs to be made."

He gave her a droll look, and Elizabeth laughed. Looking gratified, his Lordship said, "With your help, I'm sure that she can be kept on course today. Agreed?"

"Agreed," she said, very nearly in charity with him once more.

A little while after the Brimmers arrived, Lord Darvey sent a footman to request Elizabeth to accompany Lady Treadway to the salon. This was a large, nobly proportioned room done in silver and several shades of green, which gave it a cool, elegant look. It contained more furniture than the other rooms and even boasted a few objects, such as some rare seashells in a veneered Queen Anne case, whose sole purpose was to please the eye. Elizabeth thought it the prettiest room in the house.

Now, however, she did not spare a glance for any of it, so intent was she upon surreptitiously examining Lord Darvey's visitors. The grey-haired woman with the narrow, pinched face was his fiancée's mother, of course, and the plump, rather dissipated-looking blond man her brother. Elizabeth did a little shuffle, and the object of her greatest interest, seated in a shield-back chair to one side of Lord Darvey, came clearly into view.

Miss Brimmer was not beautiful, as Elizabeth had assumed she would be, but she was indeed attractive. She was dressed in a light blue paisley gown trimmed at the neck and sleeves with yellow lace. Her apparel emphasized her fragile, pale blond looks as did the faint odor of lavender that clung to her.

Her small face wore a vague, indiscriminate smile which seemed not to be directed at anyone or anything in particular. It added to her air of good-natured helplessness. Elizabeth suspected that most men would instinctively wish to protect such a young woman. It rather surprised her, though, that Lord Darvey was one of them. He seemed too independent himself to value such a trait in another.

Although she'd gotten little pleasure from it, Elizabeth's curiosity was satisfied for the time-being. Now she turned her attention back to the other occupants of the room in time to realize that Miss Brimmer's mother was staring at her.

"And who is this?" Mrs. Brimmer asked in a thin, sharp voice, pointing to Elizabeth. "I thought you said that her Ladyship's companion was to be here."

"I think that is who she must be, Mama," her daughter answered, turning her vapid smile upon Elizabeth with as much approval as she had upon the others there.

"Don't be ridiculous. Companions do not look like that."

"Miss Hanley does," Lady Treadway said loudly with unassailable logic. "You, miss," she pointed a tiny, bent finger at Miss Brimmer. "You've got a puling look. I hope you're a good breeder."

"Have a peppermint, Lady Treadway," Elizabeth said quickly, popping the confection into the other's mouth. That should keep her quiet, she thought, at least until the mint was gone. His Lordship must have had the same thought, for he gave Miss Hanley an approving wink.

Miss Brimmer smiled benignly, seeming not in the least embarrassed. "I do hope, Darvey, you mean to escort us to Lady Roody's dinner party next week. She said that you are very welcome if we let her know soon."

"Have you read *The Fifteen Plagues of a Maidenhead*?" Lady Treadway, apparently having swallowed her mint, asked no one in particular. "It's quite amusing. I'm hoping. . . ."

His Lordship's long legs shot back, and he deftly unfolded himself from his wing chair. "You look a bit weary," he said gently to his aunt, who obligingly drooped her crepey eyelids. "Would you like to return to your room for a nap now?"

Elizabeth started to inform him that her Ladyship had just had a nap, but after very little consideration, decided not to say it. Besides, she herself was eager to leave. Something about the place today oppressed her.

"Oh, must you go?" asked Miss Brimmer when Elizabeth attempted to follow Lady Treadway's chair from the room. "My mother and I mean to take a tour of the house. We'd so enjoy having you accompany us." Apparently oblivious of her mother's scowling face, she gave Elizabeth a pleasant, uncritical smile.

Miss Brimmer's brother languidly raised a plump white hand, then struggled to his feet. Encased in layers of tight clothing in various brilliant hues, Barton Brimmer made Elizabeth think of a sausage that had gone bad. He walked over toward her, a loose grin on his rouged lips. "I'm for going, too. I feel like a bit of exercise, you see. Besides, I'm rather fond of furniture and . . . uh . . . pretty things."

His host shot him an appraising look, then slowly laced his long fingers together. "You're wasting your time, Brimmer," he said icily. "I have little furniture and even less of what you refer to as pretty things. You'd have to go to the attics for those. I don't care for what's not useful, you see."

"Oh, I quite agree," said Miss Brimmer, finding a focus for her undirected smile between her fiancée's forceful, dark brows.

Mrs. Brimmer frowned at her host. "I understand that your mother had enormous collections of *objets* from China and Egypt and just about everywhere, or so I've been told." Lord Darvey nodded wryly. "I think it's most unfortunate that more of her beloved possessions have not been put on display."

"Yes, I quite agree," her daughter concurred placidly. "How I wish I could see them."

Elizabeth stared, not trusting what she'd heard. What an unusual young woman, she thought. Apparently, she said amen to everything. She certainly must have an amiable disposition—or be a fool, her own more discriminating nature insisted upon adding. She looked doubtfully at her employer, wondering if he had chosen Miss Brimmer because he loved her or merely because he desired a placable wife. If the latter were the case, he might be wise to separate her from her mother.

Lord Darvey frowned. "All of us will go to see the rooms," he said stiffly.

Omitting her bedroom and that of Lady Treadway, they visited the rooms on the first floor, leaving for last the suite that connected with Lord Darvey's bedroom. Though sparsely decorated, it was a lovely room, with its light bamboo furniture set against wallpaper printed with small flowers. Fresh white draperies at the windows and hanging from the bed's embroidered canopy added to the charm.

"I imagine this will be my room," said Miss Brimmer matter-of-factly, surprising Elizabeth with her lack of coyness. "It's very nice, isn't it, Mama?"

Since Miss Brimmer had made that same remark, or something very like, about every other chamber they'd examined, Elizabeth did not give it any significance. Instead, she waited for Mrs. Brimmer to respond to her cue and play her part.

"It will do, I suppose," said the older woman, her nostrils pinched as though she were sniffing a spoiled egg. "I cannot approve of its lack of pictures, however. A bedroom without at least four pictures, one of them depicting a country scene, cannot possibly bring relief to its weary occupant."

Miss Brimmer smiled her gentle, vacant smile. "Of course, you are right, Mama. It cannot bring relief. However, I'm sure Lord Darvey can acquire some pictures for the walls before we wed. You can, can't you?" she asked softly, focusing her gaze on her fiancé's strongly molded chin.

"Certainly, if that is what you want, my dear." His Lordship's hand lifted to pat her narrow shoulder.

Despite his reassuring gesture, Elizabeth decided that Lord Darvey did not dote on Miss Brimmer. How could he?

The satisfied feeling that thought gave her did not last longer than the time it took for her to look away. It was absurd to experience such an emotion, she silently berated herself. Whether Lord Darvey did or did not love Miss Brimmer and Miss Brimmer his Lordship could mean nothing to her. What mattered was that unless she sent information about Lord Darvey's experiments to Epsom, David would remain chained to their highly unpleasant uncle forever. Let his Lordship and that tractable ninnyhammer feel what they wished for each other. It was all one and the same to her, she told herself emphatically.

"I beg your pardon, my lord. I must have been woolgathering. I'm afraid I did not hear you." The color came up in her face as Elizabeth looked apologetically at his Lordship.

"I said . . ." Lord Darvey sounded as though he was beginning to lose patience, ". . . we've spent enough time here. Let us return to the ground floor."

Mr. Brimmer elevated one barely discernible blond brow. "Are we to see where you work? I've never known anyone who works."

"If you wish," Lord Darvey said coldly. "Come with me." Waving the other man before him, he walked out of the room, leaving the three females to follow when they would.

"Do not worry," Mrs. Brimmer said to her daughter as they walked together down the stairs. "We'll begin going through the attics tomorrow. In almost no time we can have this house arranged to our liking."

Catching the words, Elizabeth shook her head. Very likely there would be a battle of wills between Lord Darvey, with his dislike of too many possessions, and his future mama, who seemed to have other plans for his home. She wondered who would win.

When the women reached the laboratory, Elizabeth considered going to the library instead of accompanying them inside. Then she decided to follow them. She could not help but be curious about their reaction to his Lordship's specimens.

She moved off into a corner, leaving them to wander over to where Mr. Brimmer stood eyeing the rows and rows of ivory skulls. "It looks like we've stumbled upon the elephants' graveyard, doesn't it?" he said nervously, and began to giggle.

"Oh, no," his sister answered solemnly, "because then there would be tusks and things. It looks like a people's graveyard to me, and I'm afraid I don't much care for it."

His Lordship's voice was coolly polite. "How lucky for us all that you do not need to care for it, my dear, since I never take my collection from this room nor impose it upon others."

Decisively, he laid Miss Brimmer's hand upon his arm. "May I suggest that we return to the salon? You'll want to make certain you have everything before you leave." With that, he propelled her and her mother from the room.

Elizabeth sighed and turned toward the door. There was no reason for her to stay longer, either. She took a few steps but then was forced to stop. "Alone at last," said Mr. Brimmer, whose presence she had forgotten. With a speed surprising in one so round, he grabbed her right arm with one of his hands. "You smell delicious," he said, using the other hand to squeeze her firm bottom. "And you feel just wonderful."

"Good God," thought Elizabeth, stunned. "Lord Darvey was right after all. There's something about me that brings out the animal in men."

Five

ON HER WAY to meet her brother this cold and blustery morning, Elizabeth recalled her encounter in the laboratory with Mr. Brimmer two weeks before. She'd had a difficult time convincing the gentleman that she wasn't "made for love." Indeed, if one of the footmen hadn't happened to enter the room a few minutes after Brimmer put his hands on her, who could tell how that *affaire* might have concluded.

"I was probably being punished in advance," she thought with a certain moral satisfaction, "for what I'm about to do." This consisted of delivering to David her first report on Lord Darvey.

She walked down Upper Brook Street, then turned right onto Park Lane. She was dressed in tired grey half-boots, but everything else she wore was new. Her dress, her warm blue pelisse and matching bonnet, and the reticule she clutched so tightly in her right hand were all purchased with funds from his Lordship.

Elizabeth sighed. If it were for the sake of anyone other than her brother, she would turn around this instant and return to Grosvenor Square—especially before his Lordship realized that she had slipped out of the house without even informing Betsy and without, of course, taking along an escort. He wouldn't be best pleased about that.

She shook her head. She'd face that problem later. At the moment it was all she could manage not to weep over what she was doing.

Shortly, she reached the spot where her uncle's letter had told her to look for David. Indeed, he was there, but, to her confusion, he was not alone. Wrapped in a large brown garrick that she recognized as once having been the property of her uncle, he was kneeling next to a seated man clothed all in black.

Elizabeth tried to hold back a feeling of irritation, but she was not very successful. Didn't David realize, she thought apprehensively, that their business must be conducted in secrecy? She could not imagine what he was doing.

Neither of the two men seemed aware of her. Taking a step in their direction, Elizabeth called her brother's name.

Both he and his companion looked up then, and Elizabeth saw that the person in black was not, in fact, a man at all but a rather large young woman wearing a riding habit and a man's black silk top hat bent sadly out of shape.

The wintry light drawing sparks from his auburn hair, David Hanley tilted his head in a beckoning gesture and smiled at his twin. "It's all right, Liz. This young lady has had an accident. I'm helping a bit, is all."

"Thank you, but I don't need your help." The woman spoke crisply, then removed her hat and laid it on the ground. Freed from its confines, a wealth of unfashionably straight brown hair cascaded to her waist.

David's reddish brows formed a stubborn line over his eyes. "Nevertheless, I shall stay with you until your servant comes back with that runaway beast of yours or until your carriage arrives. I am David Hanley, by the way, and this is my sister, Miss Hanley. She will wait with me." He stopped frowning, to give her his wayward, unruly grin. "Won't you tell me your name?"

Elizabeth judged the woman the sort who wouldn't be impressed by David's rather intemperate charm, but she was wrong. The woman smiled, bringing about an immediate softening of her square-jawed face. "Very well." Her brown eyes twinkled. "I am Lady Thea Palmer."

David tipped his hat. "At your service, my lady."

"I do not want it." Lady Thea's voice was mock-severe. "Nobody asked you to mount guard over me, you know."

"Not true." David put up a shabbily gloved hand in a gesture of protest. "Your servant did, just before he went dashing off after your ungovernable horse."

Elizabeth coughed in order to get the attention of the combatants, who seemed to have forgotten that she was with them. "Are you all right?" she asked politely.

"If I were, would I be sitting on the ground letting this arrogant man order me about?" Any sting these blunt words might have caused was removed by Lady Thea's self-deprecating smile. "I've hurt my ankle. It's just a sprain, I'm sure, but it is rather painful, and, besides, your brother refuses to permit me to rise. I shall bring charges against you, sir."

David's only response was a wicked grin that revealed his even, white teeth.

"I do not know how you can bear him, Miss Hanley." Lady Thea accompanied this remark with a bang of her silk hat, which caused its final demise. "If he were my brother, I'd have encouraged him to move far from the nest years ago."

Elizabeth opened her mouth and then hastily closed it. She had been about to say that for the present, at any rate, she did not in fact live with her brother. A few seconds' reflection suggested it was better to leave such information unsaid. Although there was little chance that either she or her brother would ever see Lady Thea again, given their deplorable reasons for being in London, she thought it best not to pass on information about themselves.

Fortunately, the arrival of a carriage, which included the missing footman, ended the need for a response. Down stepped a physician carrying a black bag, followed by a diminutive older couple from whom issued a steady stream of clucks and cries of distress.

Since Lady Thea greeted them as *Mama* and *Papa*, Elizabeth had to assume that they were, indeed, her parents, although how such tiny, twittery people could have produced a large, stolid young woman like Lady Thea was a puzzling question. Elizabeth was reminded of two harried little wrens she had seen the past spring caring for a giant baby cuckoo which had been left to hatch in their nest by its enterprising mother.

When the patient was at last assisted to her feet, after much hand-wringing and assorted warnings of imminent disaster, Elizabeth saw that she was not as big as she'd supposed but simply large of frame and . . . well . . . sturdy-looking, like some farmer's girl. Although it was generally believed that aristocrats had a special look so that people of any rank could immediately recognize them, it had been Elizabeth's observation that while some, like Lord Darvey, did possess it, others, like her uncle and Lady Thea, did not.

Whatever her Ladyship's aspect, it was obvious to Elizabeth that Lady Thea was used to having her own way. This time she wanted order, and got it. "Mama, Papa, may I present my benefactor and his sister, Miss Hanley and Mr. Hanley. My parents," she addressed herself with an ironically tilted dark brow to Elizabeth and David, "Lord and Lady Palmer."

There were how-do-you-do's all around, and many expressions of gratitude from Lord and Lady Palmer, although none from the recipient of the care; and then Lady Thea was helped to the waiting carriage. David handed up the remains of her black top hat.

"Mama begs you to come by tomorrow morning to receive our thanks." Ignoring her silent parent's look of surprise, Lady Thea issued her invitation, which, due to her abrupt manner, came out sounding more like a command. "Say you'll come, both of you."

"Of course," said David.

"I'm afraid I cannot," Elizabeth interjected at the same time.

When her brother turned to glare his disapproval at her, Elizabeth repeated in a low voice, "I cannot," and cast an admonitory look at him. "I am sorry to decline." She turned her attention once again to Lady Thea. "But, truly, I cannot. I . . . uh . . . I have another engagement."

Lord Palmer leaned his grey head toward David. "You will still stop in to visit us tomorrow, will you not? I know you would not want to disappoint my daughter." He made a nervous sound in his throat, then scribbled his direction on a card, and, with an almost pleading look in his eyes, handed it to David.

"Hanover Square," David said, reading from the card. "I will be there." He bowed, then took his sister's arm; but instead of turning away as she expected, he kept them in that spot to stare after the departing carriage. "What a woman," he sighed. "Isn't she remarkable, Liz?"

"Yes, remarkable. I wonder if she beats her parents. No, no, David, I was only funning. It is obvious that they adore her and want only what will please her. I must say, though," she added before he could comment on her words, "that your response to their invitation took me unawares. How can you keep your promise to visit with them tomorrow? Isn't Uncle expecting you back in Epsom today?"

David's green eyes, which had been sparkling with excitement and pleasure, took on a hard, uncompromising cast. "I suppose he is, but I shan't be there. I shall be here."

"Here? That poses another problem. Where do you expect to stay?"

"Why, at Ibbetson's, probably, assuming it still has reasonable rates. Otherwise, I must throw myself upon the probably nonexistent mercies of your employer and beg a room in his attics. Or you could smuggle me inside. Would that bother you?" David smiled.

Elizabeth's pretty mouth turned down, less because of David's levity than his disparaging reference to Lord

Darvey. She had forgotten he must believe, as she used to, that his Lordship was like her uncle. Not, however, seeing any point at present in dissuading him, she directed herself to the rest of his conversation.

"I know that you are joking, David, but I am not amused. It is bad enough that I am part of Lord Darvey's household only in order to spy on him. I cannot like to think about having my accomplice in this underhanded affair take advantage of his Lordship's hospitality as well. You can understand that, can't you? Stop laughing." She raised her voice. "What I said was not meant to be entertaining."

"Wasn't it? What's wrong, Liz? It is unlike you not to see the humor in things." An arrested look replaced his easy expression. "Wait! You aren't trying to conceal something from me, are you? Has Lord Darvey been making difficulties for you?"

Elizabeth glanced at him, then turned to gaze with seeming fascination at a squirrel peering around the base of a tree. "What kind of difficulties? I do not know what you mean."

"That's it, isn't it?" David peered at her with murder in his eyes. "The man is a lecher, and he's been trying to seduce you. I shall go at once and call him out."

Elizabeth sighed. "Oh, David, he's nothing of the sort. He is a serious natural philosopher, just as Uncle said. He wants to measure skulls, not seduce me."

Unaccountably, her words brought on a feeling of depression, but she managed to keep her tone unchanged. "Furthermore, he is affianced. In sum, he's a fine, upright gentleman, and I am perfectly safe with him. I'd stake my life on that."

"That's all right, then. But I still do not see why you can't laugh about your situation. You didn't have any difficulty making a humorous remark about Lady Thea." He said this last with just a trace of petulance.

Elizabeth glared at him. "Sometimes, brother, you astonish me with your insensitivity. How can I laugh when I'm involved in a plan that calls for me to be deceitful?"

"Well, of course, you would be right, ordinarily." David gave her a cheerful smile. "But since this natural philosophy business is all a bunch of nonsense anyway, what difference does it make what you do?"

Elizabeth bowed her head. "It makes a difference to me."

"I don't like the sound of that, either." David's eyes narrowed with suspicion. "Are you becoming fond of this man, Liz?"

"Don't be absurd." Elizabeth's voice rose with unaccustomed passion. "I told you that he is affianced. Besides, I wouldn't, anyway. I'm not some foolish girl."

"I'm glad to hear it." He paused. "I say, Liz, are you sure you don't want to accept that invitation?"

So, it was back to that again. Didn't her brother understand anything? "I've already said it—I can't. I'm a companion, David. I don't have freedom to go gadding about all over town."

She would have enough trouble explaining where she had been this morning if called to account. To go off twice in two days was simply courting disaster.

"Never mind," she said more gently, seeing his contrite expression. "Let me give you this dratted letter for Uncle before I forget." Opening her reticule, she removed the folded pieces of paper.

David carelessly took the packet from her and stuffed it into a pocket, just as though, she thought, it wasn't the ticket to her damnation. "What's in it?" he asked, not sounding particularly curious. "Does it contain all of Lord Darvey's greatest secrets?"

"No, it does not." Elizabeth looked at him almost pleadingly. "I chose things that Lord Darvey doesn't care about, such as that he uses lead shot because mustard seed doesn't give an accurate measure. So, passing on this information won't actually hurt him, you see. And it is sure to help Uncle, if he will take it to heart, because it explains that what he is doing is wrong."

David laughed so unrestrainedly that Elizabeth begged him to stop. "I'm sorry." He wiped his eyes. "It's just that it all seems so ridiculous. Here we are involved in something that calls for you to pose as a companion and me to slink about in Hyde Park to get your precious information when the results were known from the start. It was hardly necessary for you to go to London to find out that Uncle is a fool. I could have told him—and everyone else—that, without your leaving Epsom."

"Shall I go home, then?" Elizabeth had not joined in the laughter, and her smile was strained. She had entered into this situation mainly for her brother's sake, and it hardly pleased her that it seemed nothing more than a silly joke to him.

His good-looking face suddenly sober, David took her arm. "I wish you would not if you can bear to stay. Remember, I'll forfeit the letter if you come home early, and, besides, I'd rather like to have the chance to go up to London more than I usually do. You know Uncle won't let me off unless it's to fetch something for him to use in his experiments or to receive your reports, as now."

When Elizabeth only pursed her mouth and did not answer, David said, "Of course, if it is too bad for you, I do not want you to stay. I'll take you back with me tomorrow, Liz."

He meant it. He was her twin brother, and she knew when he was sincere. Instead of giving him a hug, however, which was what she wanted to do, Elizabeth said mischievously, "Lady Thea and her family are quite delightful, aren't they?"

"At least one of them is." He gave her a wink from an eye as green as her own. Then, watching her smooth out a wrinkle on her pelisse, he said, "Must you go now? I shall walk you home."

"No, it won't be necessary." Elizabeth spoke hastily. Although it was time that she returned to her duties, it was better that she return alone. If any of the servants saw her accompanied by a man, they might ask more questions than they would if she came back unescorted. She could not afford to have questions asked. She was not a skillful liar; and though, thus far, she had been lucky, she could not count on her luck holding.

"I hope you have a good time tomorrow," she said with genuine feeling.

David pushed back her bonnet and planted a kiss on her cheek. "I'll let you know right after I am there. Slip out of your house about half after twelve and come across the square. I'll be waiting to tell you." With a wave of his hand, he was off, not giving her a chance to refuse.

The walk back to Grosvenor Square was almost as trying for Elizabeth as the one she'd taken to Hyde Park. Concerning the weather, which had deteriorated, it was actually worse. Or perhaps it was that now she faced into the wind, which buffeted her mercilessly. At least, fighting it kept her from thinking—almost. Over and over in her head, she heard the words from Scott's poem, "Oh, what a tangled web we weave, when first we practice to deceive. Oh, what a . . ."

". . . little beauty," a man's voice interrupted her obsessive repetition of the lines. "Come here, beauty."

Elizabeth's head, which she'd kept bent to protect her face from the wind, jerked upright. Without being aware of how far she had walked, she had come back to Grosvenor Square. In fact, she was but one house from that of Lord Darvey. It was the Brimmers' house.

Several people were congregated about the steps, all of them male and none of them anyone she had seen before. Very likely, she thought, they were known to Mr. Brimmer, although he did not make up one of their number; perhaps they were awaiting him. In any case, they were brash and rude enough to be his friends.

The man who had called to Elizabeth planted himself in

front of her, so she made to go around him. "Why be in such a hurry, sweeting?" he asked. "You won't be sorry if you stay and get acquainted with me."

Good God! Elizabeth fixed her green eyes on him. Another one who took her for a lightskirt! She shook her head at him, causing her wind-tousled russet curls to dance. "I fear you mistake the matter, sir. I belong in this neighborhood."

"That's just what I've been saying, my dear." The man put out his arms and leaned closer so that Elizabeth got a strong whiff of perspiration and stale spirits. "You belong here, with me." The arms turned into a cage.

Elizabeth looked to his friends for aid, but they were laughing and cheering him on. Now that it was too late, she wished she had obeyed Lord Darvey's edict and taken a servant with her. Unlike Epsom, in London without an escort she was apparently fair game for any man.

With iron determination, she fought her rising panic. She had to remain collected so that she could think. The man was clumsy and obviously well to go even though it was still early in the day. Perhaps she could confound him long enough to give herself the chance to escape.

"My friend is behind you," she said in what she hoped was a matter-of-fact voice. "He will not like it that you are taking liberties with me. You'd best unhand me and prepare to defend yourself."

Her jailer dropped his arms and turned. Without wasting a second, Elizabeth made for Lord Darvey's steps. She did not stop until she reached the front door. Just before she put her hand to the knocker, however, she looked back. To her astonishment, she saw that Mr. Eccleston, an expression of perplexity on his mild, innocent face, was being harangued by her erstwhile tormenter.

Along with her other crimes, was she to be responsible for embroiling Mr. Eccleston in her affairs? In considerable distress, she banged at the door.

Immediately, it opened, but instead of Hemmings' dignified face or that of one of the footmen, the countenance she saw belonged to Lord Darvey. "Your lordship." Elizabeth barely stopped herself from plunging into the haven of his arms. He was so dear, so dependable. She needed his calmness and civilized behavior.

She gazed pleadingly at him, then suddenly realized that his dark brows were drawn into angry slashes and his mouth was hard with temper. If he was calm, so, too, was a thunderstorm.

"Where were you?" he bellowed, the civilized behavior apparently having gone the way of his serenity. Ignoring her protests, he dragged her into the library.

"My lord," begged Elizabeth, needing to inform him of Mr. Eccleston's plight, "you must listen. I. . . ."

Lord Darvey planted himself in front of the white, paneled doors and spread wide his booted feet—so that she could not escape, she thought wildly. His grey eyes were like pieces of flint. "I'll ask you one more time. Where were you? And don't try to defend yourself. Tell me the truth, or it will be the worse for you."

Elizabeth could not help but object to his tone. "Your Lordship, surely you need not speak to me so."

Lord Darvey's lips tightened ominously. "Need not? I think, rather, I must. Now answer my question, for I'll brook no more delays."

If she had been more herself, most certainly Elizabeth would have attempted to placate him, but she could not bring herself to do it. He had aroused her ire, and she could not have said a soothing word to him if her very life had depended upon it.

How dare he berate her, he who had never given any indication that he was the sort who would? She simply wasn't primed for it. Besides, hadn't she suffered enough, having to sneak out, and in such unpleasant weather, in order to carry out her disreputable mission? Not to mention narrowly escaping who knew what physical indignities!

By this point, Elizabeth had given up thinking logically,

and she had forgotten Mr. Eccleston as well. Feeling tricked by life's unpredictability, not to mention its unfairness, what she wanted most was to sob into Primrose's feathers.

She wouldn't, though. Her lashes drew down over her sulky green eyes. "I have nothing further to say. May I please be excused?" Moving rapidly, she attempted to dart past the unfriendly Lord Darvey.

"Oh, no, you don't." His lordship was no clumsy tippler, like the man who had accosted her outside. He lunged quickly and grabbed hold of her, pulling her so close that his warmth enveloped her. "You aren't going anywhere until you give me some answers."

Elizabeth sucked in her breath. Lord Darvey's hard fingers, biting into the softness of her arms, were hurting her. But far worse, he was too near. His maleness was swamping her senses. "You're bruising me," she whispered and turned aside her flushed, unhappy face.

At once his Lordship's expression softened, and his fingers slid down over her arms to caress her small, cold hands. "I'm sorry. It's just that you're so pretty, I can't help but worry that someone will try to take advantage of you. Will you forgive me?"

He had said that she was pretty. Elizabeth's heart sang to joyful rhythms. Would she forgive him? Anything!

Without willing it, she moved a little closer—whereupon Lord Darvey let go of her hands and stepped back. "I worry about all of our pretty girls," he said, his glance not quite meeting hers. "You know how some men are with them. Now, if you and Betsy resembled Mrs. Mowbry, I wouldn't give your perambulations a second thought."

So much for her heart's joyful rhythms. "Men," she repeated wearily. "You are indeed right about them."

"Right? What are you taking about?" His Lordship's voice had regained its hard edge. "Has something happened? Eccleston hasn't been hanging around you again, has he?"

Good heavens. She'd forgotten about Mr. Eccleston. What an egotistical wretch she was.

Elizabeth looked at Lord Darvey beseechingly. "I do not have time to explain now, but I believe that Mr. Eccleston is presently outside Mr. Brimmer's house defending my honor. Or at least I think he is. Yes, he must be. Otherwise, he would have joined us already."

"Let me understand you." Lord Darvey's voice, though devoid of any emotion, made Elizabeth shiver. "Are you saying that because of something you did, someone has challenged my friend to a duel?"

Half-crying, Elizabeth said, "No, oh no. I'm sure it's not come to that." As his Lordship released his breath, she added with scrupulous honesty, "At least I don't think it's come to that. They may be engaging in fisticuffs, however."

"Oh, is that all?" Lord Darvey's stern expression dissolved. "You should have said so sooner."

He stepped back casually as though on his way to attend to something of little importance. If it weren't for the leaping light in his grey eyes, she would never have sensed how eager he was to join the fray. In fact, she could see that he was absolutely delighted to have an excuse to go at someone.

Her white teeth worked at her full lower lip as she pondered what was happening. Just last week she had thought to herself how well she understood Lord Darvey. It would appear that she had overstated her abilities. There were more facets to her cool, logical lord than she had assumed. Certainly, she would never have suspected that he would happily thrust himself into a public brawl.

She watched the muscles ripple across his back as he divested himself of his tight coat. She should have guessed, she thought, tugging at a wayward auburn curl. No one who traveled as he had done could be other than daring and intrepid. Nevertheless, she wished she weren't the cause of his dauntlessness this day.

His white, ruffled shirt taut across his strong shoulders, Justin Darvey turned to face her. "You," he said, "you stay where you are. We aren't finished with each other yet." Then, as lithe as a leopard, he streaked out the door.

Six

STANDING ON THE upper step of his house in the chill wind, Lord Darvey scrutinized the area around him. The square was empty except for a small knot of men standing in front of the Brimmer town house. Raising slightly on his toes, Darvey saw that the center of the knot was Mr. Eccleston. The blond-haired Eccleston was hatless, and, as was usual with him, looking rather disheveled.

Not all of the men in the group were known to Lord Darvey, but those who were did not impress him favorably. They were part of that clique of here-and-thereians who spent their time gambling, wenching, and drinking, with not a serious pursuit among them. He had nothing but contempt for them.

Which was not to say that he offhandedly dismissed them all as mere fribbles. That one over there, for example, the one with the absurd green neckcloth—Darvey often saw him working on his punches at Gentleman Jackson's, showing himself to advantage.

Lightly, Lord Darvey ran down the remaining steps and made his way over to them. "I saw you studying my cravat," the man with the green neckcloth said by way of greeting. "I am Sandor. I can tell you where to get one if you admire it."

Lord Darvey smiled blandly. "Thank you, but no thank

you; it is not precisely to my taste. Besides, I didn't come over here in order to discuss styles in cravats."

"Why did you, then?" a short man with a snub nose asked. "Who are you, anyway, and what do you want?"

What his Lordship wanted most particularly was to learn which of the men assembled had impugned Miss Hanley's honor, and he was studying what to say that would enable him to find it out. Before he could come up with a response that might elicit this information, though, another of the group, obviously continuing a conversation begun before Darvey joined them, said to Mr. Eccleston, "And I say she's no companion but a whore. Nobody ever hired a lady's companion with a mouth like that."

Aha. His Lordship smiled grimly. He thought he had his answer, and if not, it hardly mattered; this man was provoking enough to serve.

Mr. Eccleston ran a hand through his untidy blond curls. "As I've repeatedly said to you, that is truly what she is. I'll wager you wouldn't care to tell the gentleman who pays her salary otherwise." He looked toward Lord Darvey, a puckish grin acknowledging his friend's presence.

"Wouldn't I? Indeed I would," the man replied. "And if I don't get the chance, you can tell him for me."

Lord Darvey stretched out his arm and tapped the speaker on the shoulder. "How lucky for you that you do have the chance. The companion in question is a member of my household. Go on, then; tell me about her. And don't feel constrained to hold yourself back. Be as offensive as you like. It will make me enjoy so much more forcing you to your knees."

The person thus addressed was several inches taller than Lord Darvey and at least three stone more in weight. Not surprisingly, although his figure tapered to a small waist and flat stomach, he gave the impression of being heavy, especially in the upper arms and chest. On the whole, he was an impressive-looking man.

"Oh, do you think so?" He sneered at Lord Darvey. "I'm not afraid of you. I'll fight a duel with you any day."

"And cause me to have to flee the country after I've killed you?" his Lordship replied calmly. "No, thank you. Instead, I challenge you to a boxing match to be held right now in my garden. The first man to knock the other down is the winner and will accept the loser's apology."

"Don't do it, Herbert," Lord Sandor warned. "That's Justin Darvey who frequents Gentleman Jackson's. Save yourself some trouble and apologize. You don't want to go any rounds with him."

The man called Herbert thought for a few seconds and then stubbornly stuck out his chin. "It's nothing to me that he frequents Jackson's. Who doesn't? I am not worried about it."

"I strongly urge you to take my advice." Lord Sandor spoke again. "And do worry. He's not like you, Herbert. He's expert with his hands and likes to use them; I can tell. What's more, he takes the sport seriously. It's not just a fashionable pastime for him, as it is for most of us."

"I like to use my hands, too." Mr. Herbert squared off and swung his thick fist. It would have landed on his Lordship's face if he hadn't ducked so quickly.

There was a form of fighting Lord Darvey had learned in the Orient that would have brought this brute to his knees in short order, and much the worse for wear. It was too bad, he mused, that he could not now use it, but, unfortunately, it wouldn't do. He had to follow the rules of civilized society even though he didn't feel at all civilized at the moment and this group of ruffians probably never was.

"I was just playing." Herbert smiled. "Not that I don't mean to fight you. Let us go to your garden."

Once they were inside the walled enclosure, Mr. Herbert called over two of his friends and directed them to divest him of his coat. Pulling and tugging, they finally managed to do as he asked, and one of them placed it upon the branch of a lime tree. First, however, he gave Mr. Herbert a drink from an etched silver flask that had been in one of the pockets.

While this activity was going on, Lord Darvey entertained himself by staring at the back of Fidelia Brimmer's town house. He wondered if his betrothed was at home. Since he had warned her and her mother away except for certain designated days, he did not see very much of her. She did not appear to mind.

How would she react if she saw him thus? Very likely she would smile her pleasant, impartial smile and say, "I quite agree with what you are doing, Darvey, unless Mama thinks that I should quite agree with the others."

At least he'd never have to fight to defend her honor, he thought with a sardonic grin. It couldn't be impugned. No matter what anyone said to her, she would happily concur.

Loudly, Peter Eccleston cleared his throat. "Stand back, everyone. Give Darvey and Herbert some room. And if anyone else wants to fight, I'm ready to accept a challenge."

Apparently more interested in betting on the outcome of what promised to be an exciting battle between his Lordship and Mr. Herbert than in mixing it up themselves, no one bothered to respond to Mr. Eccleston's offer. They did, however, move away from the combatants as directed.

"Everything in order now?" his Lordship asked politely, and when several of the onlookers nodded, he aimed at his opponent with his left hand. It hit Mr. Herbert upon the nose.

Blood immediately spurted from the abused member onto the victim's white lawn shirt, but, thanks perhaps to the contents of the flask, he appeared not to notice and took a wild swing at Lord Darvey in turn. Out of sheer luck, it seemed, it struck his Lordship's shoulder. "That's one for me," he crowed as Justin staggered. His bosom friends cheered.

His face expressionless, Lord Darvey let fly once more, this time with his right hand, and connected with Mr.

Herbert's chin. The blow should have felled an ox, but Mr. Herbert barely wavered. One of his Lordship's dark eyebrows lifted a quizzical fraction.

During the next ten minutes, Lord Darvey continued to hit his opponent with a lightning series of left-handed jabs and right-handed hard punches, none of which seemed to have any effect. He, himself, ducked every blow directed his way in a magnificent display of bobbing and weaving. Since neither man seemed able to best the other, it looked as though the fight might go on forever.

In fact, his Lordship felt himself tiring. He needed to dispatch the lummox opposite him shortly, or he, Darvey, might end up lying defeated on the ground. That would be intolerable. He was fighting for Elizabeth's honor; he must not lose.

Using all of his strength, he directed his fist to his adversary's stomach. It landed with a thud—followed immediately by what sounded like an explosion. Like some giant tree, Mr. Herbert swayed, then listed, then fell. Unmoving, he lay in a tangled heap at Justin Darvey's feet.

"Stap me," whispered one of the onlookers in an awestruck voice. "Lord Darvey has shot Bob."

"What are you talking about, you muttonhead?" his Lordship said irritably. "I said I wouldn't fight a duel, didn't I? Of course, I did not shoot him. I didn't even bring a gun.

"Get up, you damn fool," he commanded Herbert, prodding him ungently with the toe of his boot. But his foe did not respond.

"Somebody shot him," the man said stubbornly. "I heard the gun go off; we all did." Like a set of mechanical toys, Mr. Herbert's friends turned as one to glare at Peter Eccleston.

"Don't look at me," he exclaimed indignantly. "I don't have one, either. And even if I did, I wouldn't use it in a bout of fisticuffs. No gentleman would."

At this point, Mr. Herbert groaned, and everyone's attention shifted back to him. "Herbert." The snub-nosed man bent over him. "Are you all right? Where did he get you?"

"Never mind that." Mr. Herbert spoke between gasps. "Just help me up. But be careful how you do it; I think I've snapped in two."

The snub-nosed man backed off with a horrified look. "I can't help you. I might get blood on my clothes."

"There isn't any blood, you clunch. I wasn't shot."

His friend's face wore an expression of disbelief. "Are you sure? We heard the gun go off, you know."

"I don't care what you heard." Mr. Herbert was clearly exasperated. "I say I wasn't shot, and I ought to know."

Lord Darvey looked down at his erstwhile opponent. "Tell us what happened, then. Although I'd like to take the credit for your fall, I have a feeling that I wasn't really responsible."

"But you were." Mr. Herbert's voice sounded strangled. "In a way."

Lord Darvey edged a bit nearer. "I don't take your meaning. Could you be more explicit?"

Mr. Herbert muttered indistinctly, causing his Lordship to cup his ear and lean closer. "I said," the beleaguered Herbert suddenly roared, "you made my corset burst, and the stays are sticking me something fierce. I'm skewered, is what I am. Now, are you satisfied?"

"Yes," said Lord Darvey, nodding gravely. Then he clutched his middle and began to laugh.

He was still laughing when he and Mr. Eccleston walked around to the entrance of his town house. "It was an unusual fight," Mr. Eccleston commented as they stood on the pavement talking, "the most unusual one I've ever seen. I don't remember Herbert apologizing, though. Did he apologize?"

"No, but there was no need." Lord Darvey sounded his usual tolerant self once more. "Seeing him sprawled on the ground like that was apology enough—that and having the fight stop. I tell you truly, Eccleston, I'm not sure how much longer I could have kept it up."

"Oh, is that so? I would never have guessed it. At any rate, you were grand. Congratulations."

"Thank you, but I fear I don't deserve them. I didn't win. Old Herbert's corset did." He chuckled. "The next time I fight a fat opponent with a magnificently flat stomach, I'll know what's up."

Mr. Eccleston frowned. "The next time? Are you planning to make a career of defending Miss Hanley's good name?"

"No, of course not." Darvey flushed. "I don't know what I was thinking of when I said that. It was pretty good sport though, wasn't it?"

Mr. Eccleston grabbed his friend's shoulder and gave it an affectionate squeeze, causing his Lordship to wince. "Sorry." He grinned sheepishly. "I forgot that was where he hit you. To answer your question, yes, it was the best. But it's made me devilish sharp-set. Do you think I might have something to eat?"

"Anything you want." His Lordship began laughing again, and the two friends entered the house.

Once inside, and having given his order for a meal for Mr. Eccleston, Lord Darvey seemed to suffer a rapid change of mood. "I just remembered that I have something to attend to," he said brusquely. "Why don't you take yourself off to the dining room, and I'll join you shortly."

"What do you have to attend to? Can't I go with you? I don't understand what could be so important that it can't be put off." Spouting questions and comments, Mr. Eccleston trailed behind his friend. Shrugging, his Lordship let him enter the library with him.

Elizabeth, as directed, had been waiting there the whole time. It had been an interminable wait, made worse by visions of Lord Darvey, his handsome face battered and bloodied, lying stretched out unconscious on the ground. Although she had tried to give an occasional thought to Mr.

Eccleston, too, of course, her chief concern had been for his Lordship; she could not seem to help herself.

She looked up when the men entered the room, her green eyes going hungrily to Lord Darvey's face. "Thank God," she exclaimed. "You're safe. I am so happy." So saying, she began to cry.

Lord Darvey tried to hold on to his anger, but he could feel it melting under Elizabeth's tears. He turned up his hands, admitting defeat. Then he walked to where she stood and put his arms about her. "My dear girl," he said rather desperately, "please don't cry. It's all right, I promise."

Murmuring something unintelligible, Elizabeth snuggled against him. "There, there." His lips nuzzled her russet curls.

Unfortunately, this behavior seemed to make her feel worse, for she cried even harder. Not knowing what else to do, Lord Darvey tightened his grasp.

She certainly had splendid breasts, he thought distractedly. They were burning two holes in his chest. And she smelled just wonderful, like . . . he wasn't sure exactly what it was but it made him want to bury his head in her creamy neck and. . . . Lord Darvey's lean form grew rigid. In heaven's name, what was he thinking of?

"You'll be fine," he said unsteadily. "Won't she, Eccleston?" For the first time since they had come into the room, he looked at the other man.

Mr. Eccleston had been standing to one side this whole while, staring in fascination at his best friend hugging Lady Treadway's companion. "Yes, fine." Nervously, he cleared his throat. "Nothing to it. Darvey routed them all."

His Lordship released his hold on Elizabeth and walked over to join him. "Come now," he said, sounding relieved, "I only had one to contend with. You had the whole lot." He laughed uneasily, then pounded Mr. Eccleston on the back. "Tell me, what did you think of my footwork? Do you think Gentleman Jackson would have approved?"

After several moments of noisy discussion on this apparently intriguing topic, his Lordship looked behind him to where he'd left Elizabeth. She was not there, having gone out through the door leading to the laboratory.

"Well, well," said Mr. Eccleston.

His Lordship frowned. "And what is that supposed to mean?"

"Oh, nothing." Mr. Eccleston gave him a conciliatory smile. "I must say, though, that it surprised me when Miss Hanley cried. She had not struck me as the watering pot sort."

Remembering his cavalier treatment of her earlier in the day, Lord Darvey flushed. "I imagine most women are if pushed to it."

"Is that so? Who pushed her?"

His Lordship looked evasive. "I don't know that anybody did, actually. She implied that she was worried about us, didn't she? That's probably the explanation."

"Worried about you, don't you mean?" Mr. Eccleston chuckled. "I think she's fond of you, Darvey. And I think you're fond of her."

Lord Darvey stiffened, but when he spoke his voice was as neutral as though the topic under discussion was the weather. "I cannot answer for Miss Hanley," he said, "but as for myself, certainly I am fond of her. I have a fondness for all of my staff. I'd think myself a poor sort of employer if I didn't."

"I do not doubt a word you say, dear chap," Mr. Eccleston responded soothingly. "It's just that seeing you give . . . ah . . . comfort to her, I had an idea."

If he expected encouragement from Lord Darvey, he was doomed to disappointment, for his Lordship's face wore a most forbidding frown. Nevertheless, Mr. Eccleston persevered. "Do you remember when I suggested that you make her your wife and you rejected the suggestion? Now, I have a better idea. Got it from old Herbert, as a matter of fact. I think you should make her your mistress. Well, what do you think?"

"I think you've taken leave of your senses." His Lordship spoke through clenched teeth. "Even if Miss Hanley were willing, which I feel certain she is not, I am not willing. I do not want a mistress, Eccleston. What I want is a well-ordered existence so that I can finish my report to the Royal Society. And what I want even more than that is not to have to listen to idiotic suggestions from people who should know better."

"But. . . ."

"There is no but. I tell you unequivocally, Eccleston, I have no desire to make Miss Hanley my mistress. She doesn't appeal to me that way, and, besides, if you will but stop to remember, I am engaged to be married. I have no use for another female in my life."

Turning his back to his friend, Darvey stared across the room. He was caught up in a monumental effort to recollect his fiancée's face, something he never was able to do. At this point, however, he felt it was essential to succeed. By concentrating intently, he was able to capture a brow here and an angular curve there, but to save his life he could not seem to put the separate parts together. He had no trouble conjuring up a detailed picture of Miss Hanley, though. A fine sprinkle of perspiration covered his brow.

Blast Peter Eccleston, and blast Elizabeth Hanley. "I am going to my room," he announced coldly. "I suggest that you repair to the dining room and have your meal. After that, you may go home." His heels pounding the gleaming, uncarpeted floor, Lord Darvey exited the room.

A short while later he was soaking in his tub. The heat should help his aching shoulder, he thought, peering through the steam. Would that it could help his muddled thoughts.

It had been a very emotional day, and he did not like emotion. Well, at least, he did not trust it; it could easily lead one astray. Logic was better.

Alas, that seemed to have deserted him, and he wondered

what was happening to him. Wearily, he sank farther down into the water while he pondered the question.

His difficulties had to do with Miss Hanley; that was obvious. With *Elizabeth*. That he had some strong feeling for her was undeniable, no matter what he'd told Eccleston. As for Miss Brimmer, he tolerated her, but that was all. That was why he had chosen her. He needed to concentrate on his work.

"Oh, hell." With a scowl, he stepped from the tub and carelessly wrapped himself in his banyon. His skin still glistening with moisture where the garment left him bare, he stepped into his bedroom.

A sound, a tiny gasp, made Lord Darvey look up. "What are you doing here?" he asked Elizabeth sharply, more sharply than he meant.

Instead of answering, she gasped again and let a small picture in a gold frame fall from her hand. It tumbled to the floor.

"I'll get it." Lord Darvey crouched down to retrieve a painted likeness of his great aunt when she was young. The posture caused his robe to part, revealing one long, hair-roughened thigh.

"Oh, my." There was a look almost of terror on Elizabeth's pallid face. "Her Ladyship insisted that I put this in your room, but I think I should come back later. I mean, there's no reason to come back at all . . . or stay."

Of course, she should go. It was dangerous for both of them for her to be alone with him like this. "Don't leave." Lord Darvey's voice was thick. "Tell me why she decided that I should have it now."

"Why, I don't know." Elizabeth edged closer to the door. "She can be whimsical at times."

His Lordship laughed. "Indeed, she can be, and several other adjectives as well."

Oh, dear, he was pleasant. How dreadful. Elizabeth sidled a bit nearer the outside door. It was not that she did not trust his Lordship to remain a gentleman, for, of course, she did. It was that she feared the more intimate setting, unlike the laboratory, might make her feel awkward about being alone with him. Indeed, it did make her feel awkward.

"Well, I'd best be off now." She sighed nervously. "For some reason, things are out of kilter today, her Ladyship's nap time and just everything. I don't know why."

She didn't know why? That was a foolish remark. She was very much aware of the reason everything was at sixes and sevens this day; it was her fault.

"I never thanked you for defending my name," she said, for the first time since entering the room looking directly into his eyes. "I am excessively obliged to you, your Lordship."

Apparently forgetting that he was not dressed as he should be, or, indeed, hardly dressed at all, Lord Darvey sat himself upon the bed. "Then tell me where you were this morning," he said, to Elizabeth's surprise.

She gave him an inquiring look before saying, "I went to Hyde Park to meet my brother."

"Is that true? That's all right, then. But why didn't you tell me?" When Elizabeth only hung her head and did not answer, as had happened before Lord Darvey supplied an answer for her. "I suppose you didn't think it necessary since you were going just a short way and to visit a relative." His voice deepened. "But you know better now, don't you?"

Indeed, she did, she thought. She knew better than to keep looking at the exposed portions of his body. He was beautiful, so very beautiful, with all that sleek, bare skin. She had not realized that men were made so fine. A strange warmth spread down her limbs.

Against her will, she peered at him once more. His torso, outlined by the damp cloth clinging to him, was long and sinuously lean except for where knots of muscles stood out. Unlike her own body, there was a quantity of hair on his chest, dark and wet from his bath. It looked to be shaped rather like a kite, she thought, with its string ending somewhere under his robe. She found herself wondering how far the string extended. She wished that she could see.

This time, the heat from her blush nearly scalded her. Oh, lord, she was abandoned. "Dissolute jade," she castigated herself fiercely. "You are no different from Mr. Brimmer."

Perhaps Lord Darvey caught the direction of her long-lashed eyes. More likely, he noticed her crimson skin. In any case, he pulled the banyon more closely about himself. "I beg your pardon. Now I am more respectable, I hope."

Indeed, he was. The problem was that she was not. All she'd felt when he covered himself was disappointment. She had not wanted to stop looking yet. In fact, she could have gazed and gazed again. Almost certainly, she belonged in bedlam, and very probably she was damned.

"I am without morals," she decided sadly. "It was not enough that I am here as a spy, but I must needs be a wanton as well. It is little wonder that I elicit lowering remarks."

With a start, she realized that his Lordship was addressing her. "I beg your pardon, my lord." She blushed once more. "I must have been thinking of something else; I am afraid that I did not hear you."

"I said that the next time your brother comes to town, you must invite him to stay with us."

Elizabeth shuddered. What a dreadful idea. If the two men met, very likely her brother would insult Lord Darvey by giving his opinion of people who measure skulls, or else he'd forget and reveal that they were related to Lord Beowulf. Neither thought was comforting.

"Actually, I'm to see him tomorrow," she confessed, thinking it best to do so. "We'll meet just across the square for a few minutes, with your permission." Lord Darvey nodded. "Since he will be in a hurry to get home, I shall not bother to bring him here and introduce him. Another time." Her voice trailed off into vagueness.

"As you wish. Just be certain to take Betsy with you. If being but one house away is dangerous, just think how fraught with peril venturing across the square might be." He smiled at her.

Not as perilous as staying here longer with you, she thought, and quickly made her excuses. This time his Lordship did not try to detain her.

Once free from Lord Darvey's disturbing presence, she raced down the hall to her room. If she did not hasten to unburden herself to Primrose, she thought, she'd not be able to bear it. He would probably scold her quite severely, no doubt, but that was no more than she deserved.

With her pet perched upon her hand, Elizabeth climbed up onto her walnut four-poster. "I think we should have stayed in Epsom," she advised the little bird as she leaned back carefully upon her pillows. "For David's sake, too. I fear he is entertaining ideas that might make him want to reach too high."

The canary opened his little beak and sang a few brittle notes. "Wait," Elizabeth said. "You haven't heard the half." She bent her head so that her auburn curls almost touched his bright feathers. "There's no need to go into the reasons, but the fact is that twice today I felt certain stirrings that I do not believe a lady, or even a companion, is ever supposed to feel. The first time was when his Lordship held me, and the second was when I saw him after his bath. Oh, my dear, he was so beautiful."

The canary moved restlessly upon her hand, but caught up in her emotions, Elizabeth did not notice. "I do not mean to use aesthetics as an excuse, you understand. I'm sure I should never have felt what I did, which was lust, Primrose—yes, lust, though I know I shouldn't even say the word."

Primrose cautiously extended his wings and stood teetering on her hand. "Won't you please be still until I have finished?" Elizabeth sounded aggrieved. "And try to have a little compassion for me—although I cannot have any for myself. This is not easy for me, you know.

"It's just that when I saw his Lordship's bare skin and manly. . . ." She paused and flung wide her arms.

"Primrose. Oh, Primrose." Elizabeth slid hastily from the bed.

Lying upon his back on the floor, his spiky little legs sticking straight up, the little yellow ball did not respond with even a single chirp. "Oh, my God," Elizabeth wailed, looking down with eyes filled with fear. "My unnatural longings have killed him."

She raised her eyes to the ceiling. "If he recovers, I'll never think of his Lordship like that again; I swear it."

Rushing into the hall, she found Mrs. Mowbry, who with a judicious drop of brandy brought Primrose around. "Thank you, oh, thank you, for giving us another chance," she said to the uncomprehending woman. "I've learned my lesson."

Of course, she had. She was a rational woman, not some foolish, giddy moth. She was not willing to be burned up in the flames for the sake of a bit of heat.

And yet, a traitorous voice inside her whispered, a life without heat would provide cold comfort, indeed.

Enough! She would make herself think of other things. With a last worried look in her small friend's direction, she went to the library to look for something improving to read, not only for Lady Treadway's sake but also her own.

Seven

ALTHOUGH ELIZABETH DID not know it, during this time Justin Darvey was also treating himself with brandy. Usually, he was not much of an imbiber because he felt that alcohol dulled his mind. Now, however, he had decided that some dulling might be just the thing.

Leaning back upon his thick bed pillows, he poured himself a glass from the bottle he'd had the footman bring. Then he held the crystal goblet away to watch the light play with the drink's rich, luscious colors. The colors reminded him of Elizabeth's hair. He knew he should resist thinking about her hair, or any other part of her, but he found that he could not. Very well, then, he thought tiredly. "To Elizabeth's hair."

He held the brandy in his mouth for a minute, to warm it, then let it slip down his throat. It went like liquid silk. Elizabeth's skin must feel like that. "To Elizabeth's skin." He tilted his goblet more readily now.

By the time he finished saluting each of her facial features, neck, breasts, and navel, he was unmistakably befuddled. "I'm as drunk as a lord," he told himself with owllike seriousness, "or is that, I am drunk and a lord?" No matter; either way, the expression fit.

Feeling suddenly sleepy, Lord Darvey set his goblet on the small table next to his bed. Wearily, he sank farther into the pillows and closed his eyes. How pleasant it would be to rest for just half an hour, he thought.

And all of a sudden there was Elizabeth, standing inside the door. Firelight licked her white skin. Slow-thighed, she walked toward him, rolling her slender hips. Her rounded arms were extended as though she could not bear to wait to connect with him. She was totally, gloriously, nude.

She lay down beside him on the counterpane and shifted her pale, shapely limbs. Her green eyes were hot and eager, her red mouth an open invitation.

Justin leaned over her and kissed her mouth, once and again. Then he covered her eyes and cheeks with kisses. His lips moved down her neck to her shoulders. They were soft and smelled of good things like oranges and brandy and the perfume made from roses that she favored. He kissed the hollows of her shoulders and let his tongue taste all of the good things.

Her breasts were high and firm and whiter than her face. He kissed them. Then, gently, ever so gently, so that Elizabeth would continue to trust him and not be afraid, he slid his hands down the sleek slope of her belly.

Some burning logs shifted and fell noisily in the fireplace. There was a shower of blue and gold sparks. His Lordship awoke. His hand went to where Elizabeth should have been, but there was no warm, willing body there. Indeed, the place where he thought she lay was cool. The sweet cheat was gone.

Unwillingly, he opened his eyes and sat up. He had been dreaming. Elizabeth had not been beside him, nor would she ever be. He would not stroke her skin or see her bare, pink-tipped breasts and rounded hips. He would never feast from the hollows of her shoulders.

He ran a careless hand through his usually disciplined black locks. He wanted her. If he hadn't precisely accepted that fact before, he had to now. But he knew that he wasn't going to get her. For him, there would only be Fidelia Brimmer and family. Reason had made him miscalculate badly it seemed. With a curse, his Lordship picked up the crystal goblet and threw it into the fire. Then he vowed to keep his distance from Elizabeth.

After her shattering experience with him and with Primrose, Elizabeth was just as willing as he. Thus, Lord Darvey found it comparatively easy to keep his word to himself. If the Prince Regent hadn't asked him to give a reception for some visiting German astronomers, Darvey might well have done so for two or three days altogether.

The problem was his housekeeper, Mrs. Mowbry. When he tried to convince her that she could manage such an affair herself, she said, "I can live with your skulls, if I must, my lord, but what I can't deal with is princes and Germans. I'm giving my notice." Not until he promised to have Elizabeth assist her did she agree to stay at her post.

Now all he had to do was to convince Elizabeth. To that end, he bade her attend him in the library. "I have decided to have a reception here for members of the Royal Society," he said, "and I would like you to help Mrs. Mowbry with the details. Lady Treadway has given her approval. What is the matter?" he asked anxiously. "You look pale."

"I—I'm—pray, who will be coming?" Elizabeth's voice shook.

His Lordship could not keep himself from patting her hand. "Do not worry. It is just a small affair for my friends in the Society." He grinned apologetically. "And the Prince Regent."

If he was inviting his friends, that meant that her uncle would definitely not be there. Elizabeth smiled weakly. Now all she had to worry about was assisting in arranging an evening fit for a prince.

As it turned out, she need not have worried. The Prince Regent sent his regrets. Thus, the night of the reception her duties consisted of nothing more than soothing Mrs. Mowbry and encouraging the cook. At least that was true until one of the guests tore his coat and she was pressed into service to mend it.

She followed a footman to the library where the owner of the coat was sitting in his shirtsleeves and gaudy green brocade vest, his chair half-turned to the wall. Elizabeth made a little noise to get his attention, then curtsied and extended her hand for the damaged garment. When she saw who occupied the chair, however, she immediately let her arm drop.

"What are you doing here?" She addressed her uncle in a horrified tone.

Lord Beowulf gave his niece a crafty, self-satisfied smile, like some feline who, heaven forbid, had just eaten the canary. "I am putting in an appearance at Darvey's reception, of course. What do you think I am doing?"

"Since you were not invited, Uncle, I am sure I do not know. You must leave at once before Lord Darvey sees you."

Lord Beowulf grinned at his niece. "He already saw me and did nothing. That is lucky for him, because I have no intention of leaving. I mean to stay here as long as I wish and then go off with Cranley. I shan't return to Epsom until tomorrow some time. Now, get on with it, girl, and fix my coat."

Elizabeth looked at him with suspicion. "Is it really torn?" When he thrust the antique satin garment toward her so that she could see that it was ripped up one side, she said, "It wouldn't surprise me if you had torn it yourself in the hope of getting me in here with you." Noting his sly grin, she realized she had guessed the truth. "You are disgraceful, Uncle. I will not talk to you anymore tonight, nor will I mend your coat."

"Indeed, you'll do both." His raspy voice was angry. "Else I shall go and tell that fool Darvey why you are really here."

Elizabeth looked at him skeptically. "You won't tell him; that would make no sense."

"That wouldn't stop me," he said, causing her to dimple involuntarily. "I might do it just to get you back home before you're completely ruined. It seems to me that you've become far too cocky for your own good and forgotten your place. Being in this house has done something to you."

Indeed, it had, far more than he dreamed or that she could tolerate thinking about just then.

Wearily, she sat down near him and reached out her hand. "Give me the coat. But do not talk overmuch to me. I would not want people to get the impression that we are on terms of familiarity."

Lord Beowulf's full-jowled face set stubbornly. "No one here but Cranley knows that we are related. I shall talk as much as I please. I'll go where I please, too," he added. "I've already been once to Darvey's laboratory, you know, and may go again, although it's a poor excuse for such a place." He ended his remarks with a sneer.

Although she knew she was being foolish, Elizabeth felt stung by her uncle's criticism of his Lordship. How dare he find fault with that laboratory!

"And what is wrong with it?" she asked with a haughty toss of her reddish curls.

Before answering, her uncle made little pushing movements with his fingers toward the coat she held to remind her to continue to get on with her mending. It made her want to throw the garment to the floor and jump on it.

"Fah. It's a woman's room, all neat and tidy, with everything in its little place, the skulls on the shelves and Darvey's manuscript for the Royal Society in the desk. Right? Isn't that where it is?"

Elizabeth's eyes narrowed with suspicion. "It's certainly no concern of yours where his manuscript is. If I were you, Uncle, I'd worry about using mustard seed rather than lead shot instead of thinking about his Lordship's paper."

"Is that a fact? Since when have you become an expert on my life's work?" Lord Beowulf's voice dripped with scorn. "You are a woman and know nothing."

Elizabeth's mouth compressed tightly. She was not used to hearing her sex maligned since coming into his Lordship's household. In fact, since becoming Lord Darvey's assistant, she had received more than her share of praise for her abilities. It made her very angry to have to be subjected again to her uncle's misanthropy. "I won't listen to that sort of talk anymore, Uncle. You may say that all men are smarter than women, but I know now that I have more intelligence than quite a few men I have met."

"Is that a fact?" Uncle Beowulf sneered. "And I say that cannot be true. But if it is . . ." He interrupted his words to laugh contemptuously. "If it is, the explanation is obvious."

Elizabeth looked up, her green eyes cold. She knew she would not like what she was about to hear.

"Since women cannot by their nature be more intelligent than men, there's only one conclusion to be drawn. You are not a woman. No more need be said."

Why did she bother to talk to him? Furious, Elizabeth got up from her chair and began rapidly walking away.

"My coat, missy." Lord Beowulf ran after her. "Give me my coat."

Elizabeth looked down at the shabby garment, the needle and thread still dangling from where she had stitched. Grabbing hold of the needle, she tugged so that the part of the coat she had mended gaped open once more. "I suggest that you go home, Uncle," she said sweetly. "You are obviously not fit to be seen."

"Why, you little jade." His face as red as his hair, Lord Beowulf lifted his beefy hand to strike his niece.

"I say, what's going on here?" asked Peter Eccleston, who chanced to glance into the library as he was strolling by.

"Why, nothing," said Elizabeth. "You must excuse me; I am wanted somewhere else." She directed a poisonous glare at her uncle, then curtsied to Mr. Eccleston and left.

Despite Mr. Eccleston's efforts to interrogate him, Lord

Beowulf departed the room as well. The younger man lost sight of his Lordship after that until he heard his supercilious voice at the center of a group of natural philosophers. The person Beowulf was addressing was their host.

"You will agree that the cranial cavity gives an accurate measure of the brain it once held, will you not?" Beowulf sounded like a schoolmaster quizzing a student who had failed to do his lessons. At Darvey's indifferent nod, he continued, "Thus, a large cavity means the skull once contained a large brain, isn't that so?" Again, his Lordship nodded without bothering to answer.

"Then why won't you agree that Anglo Saxons and Teutons have the largest brains and Jews, Hindus, and the rest of that sort are below them—with women and children on the bottom, of course?"

There was a scattering of applause and a chorus of "Here, here" from some of the guests.

Lord Darvey patted his mouth with a large, tanned hand as though to conceal a yawn. "Come and listen to me read my paper at the April meeting," he said. "I will deal with those matters then." So saying, he turned his back on his uninvited guest and made his way to Sir Joseph Banks, who was holding court near the door.

"Popinjay," Lord Beowulf muttered as his audience began to drift off in the wake of their host's abrupt leave-taking. "We'll see who has the final word."

Although no longer the center of attention, he continued to remain at the reception until very late. Indeed, quite a few of the guests did. Thus, it was some time before the staff were free to go to their beds. Elizabeth was so exhausted by then that she had stopped worrying about what mischief her uncle might be planning and was interested solely in reaching her own rooms before she collapsed.

When she finally did go upstairs, she just managed to don her night clothes and perform her ablutions before falling upon her mattress. Then she slid into a deep sleep.

It seemed but a few minutes later that an urgent hand

shook her awake. "Miss Hanley." Lord Darvey's deep voice penetrated her unconscious state. "You must wake up and come to the library with me. There is something we need to discuss."

"Tomorrow," she groaned, still too somnolent to realize that it was hardly the thing for her to remain snuggled in her feather bed while his Lordship was in her room. Indeed, it was hardly the thing for him to be there at all, but her befogged brain didn't take that in, either. "Too tired now."

Strong hands propped her against her pillows. "I am truly sorry, but I'm afraid you must do as I ask. Come, I will help you." Taking up her old printed cotton robe, which he found by the light of an oil lamp he'd set near her bed, he got her arms into the sleeves. Next, he picked her up and set her upon her feet.

"Umm," said Elizabeth and promptly sank against him. Her round, high breasts pressed against his chest.

"Don't do that." The sharp note in His Lordship's voice finally brought her awake. "It's been difficult enough, and then seeing you and holding you . . .   Stand up, Miss Hanley, do."

Fully awake at last, Elizabeth was now more than eager to comply. She pulled away, almost falling in her haste to escape. Unlike her, Lord Darvey was fully clothed. Still, through the layers he wore, she had felt his hard chest. Her awareness of it, of the whole wonderful, muscled length of his body, made her uneasy.

"Fine. Now pick up your right foot." Except for a certain edginess, Lord Darvey could have been talking to an uncomprehending child. "No, not that one. Never mind." Bending down, he forced a slipper onto Elizabeth's left foot; then he maneuvered her into the other. Taking up the lamp, he grasped her hand and led her into the hall.

The cooler air there was like a blow. It shook off any remaining cobwebs in her brain. "What is it?" she asked anxiously, curiosity finally uppermost in her mind. "Has something happened to Lady Treadway or to one of the staff?"

"I will explain it to you when we get to the library." His Lordship lifted the lamp to light the way. "Eccleston is there, and we wish to talk about a matter with you."

She wanted to ask why it could not wait until the morning, but something held her back. Stumbling behind him, she followed him down the stairs.

There was a chair drawn up across from the blue sofa Mr. Eccleston sat upon. When he saw her, he waved her to it, his boyish features unnaturally severe. "Now, Miss Hanley, we need to ask you some questions, and it is of the utmost importance that you tell us the truth."

"Just a minute, Eccleston," his Lordship interrupted. "There's no need for you to take that tone with her. There's no need for you to say anything at all, in fact. Miss Hanley is a member of my household, and, therefore, it is my responsibility to question her."

Looking chagrined, Mr. Eccleston slumped back against the sofa cushions. "Very well, if you wish. Still, I think that I should be permitted to say something."

"If it becomes necessary, then you may. Otherwise, please don't."

What did all of this mean? Elizabeth could not make anything of the interchange between the two men. And what was she doing there in the middle of the night dressed in a thin robe that barely kept her from freezing? Unable to control herself, she shivered.

"You're cold." Although obviously preoccupied with something, his Lordship sounded concerned. Taking off his coat, he slipped it over her shoulders. It was warm from his body and had the tantalizingly masculine odor that Elizabeth associated with him. She shivered again, but not, this time, from the cold.

"I'll build up the fire." Despite her assurance that it was unnecessary, Lord Darvey stirred it with a poker and then added several logs.

All this time, Mr. Eccleston had been tapping his fingers on the arm of the sofa. "If you've run out of things with which to busy yourself, Darvey, do you think we might get to the questions? It is late, you know."

"Yes, I think we are ready now. Miss Hanley . . . Elizabeth . . . I have shocking news. Except for a few pages, my manuscript is missing, and we can only conclude that it was taken by one of my guests."

The sickness of exhaustion Elizabeth felt before was nothing compared to the sickness she experienced now. Could her uncle have stolen Lord Darvey's work? She could not bear to believe it.

"Have you looked carefully for it?" she asked in a voice of eager desperation. "Did you put it somewhere different, perhaps, to keep it out of the guests' way? You might have done that and then forgotten where you set it."

"No, I did not." Although his Lordship's face now wore its usual inexcitable expression, his grey eyes bespoke his concern. "In fact, I considered doing that but then decided against it for the very reason you just gave. I locked the desk, of course, but our enterprising thief managed to get it open." He laughed, but there was nothing of humor in the sound.

Elizabeth got up from her chair. "Could it still be in the drawer somewhere? I could go now and look for it."

"Thank you, but I assure you that it isn't there. Besides the few pages that were left behind and a length of thread, the drawer is empty."

Elizabeth's creamy skin lost the little color it had previously had. "Thread?" she stammered.

"Yes." Lord Darvey shrugged, apparently not considering its presence significant.

"It isn't on any of the shelves in the laboratory, either," Mr. Eccleston said. "Nor is it in the library."

His Lordship nodded. "I assure you that we checked most carefully, Miss Hanley. No, I'm afraid that essentially my manuscript is gone." He hesitated. "Eccleston said he saw you here in the library at one point talking to Lord Beowulf. We were wondering if he said anything that would make you suspect he might have been up to some mischief."

Elizabeth started to tremble. She did not know what to say. Although she could truthfully answer in the negative to Lord Darvey's question, she no longer doubted that her uncle was the thief.

"No, of course, he didn't." Noticing her disturbed state, his Lordship answered his own query, then briefly put his arm about her and gave her a reassuring squeeze.

Mr. Eccleston looked nonplussed. "Just a minute," he said, then subsided when Lord Darvey turned to glare at him.

"I am so sorry," said Elizabeth, mechanically winding and unwinding the sash of her robe around her wrist. "What shall you do? Does it mean that you will not be able to read your paper?"

"I suppose that whoever took it would like that, but, no, I do not think that will happen. Remember, I still have all of my computations in the brown ledger; thank heavens the thief didn't know about that. I shall have to work very hard, of course, to rewrite everything and finish my measurements. I'll need your help, Miss Hanley. With it, I think I can get the paper done on time."

Elizabeth took several steps toward him. "Anything; I'll do anything to assist you. We can start now." Forgotten was her debilitating weariness. All she wanted was to aid the man she loved.

The dim room suddenly became luminous. Elizabeth felt herself drenched in joy. She loved Lord Darvey! She loved him! How could she not have known it? She wanted to skip, to laugh, to sing. With love-dazzled eyes she looked up at him. "Did . . . did you say something?"

His Lordship appeared not to notice anything out of the way. "Yes, I said that later in the morning will be soon enough." He seemed to be about to dismiss her, and Elizabeth half-turned toward the door. She was eager to get to her room, but not to sleep. She had much that was lovely to think about. She gave him a blinding smile.

"Just a minute." Mr. Eccleston put out his hand to stay her. "I'd still like to know what passed between you and Lord Beowulf. It seemed dashed queer. For a minute, I thought he might hurt you."

How could anybody or anything hurt her? She had found her one true love! "I was only mending his coat," she said dreamily. "You are mistaken, sir."

"She was mending his coat," said his Lordship. "I knew it must be something like that. She does not even know the man."

As quickly as it had come, her giddy elation left her. Lord Darvey was wrong. She did know the man. He was her uncle, and she was a spy for him. And the person she was spying on, the person she loved above all things, was betrothed. She might have just acknowledged to herself the depth of her feeling for Lord Darvey, but otherwise nothing had changed.

Her green eyes now held such a look of hopelessness that Lord Darvey could not bear to see it. Giving her a little push in the direction of the hall, he said, "Go back to bed, Miss Hanley. I am sorry that I roused you."

When the door had closed behind her defeated-looking figure, he turned back to his friend. "I told you that she knew nothing. I was a fool to let you convince me to wake her. The poor thing is dropping."

"I don't know, Darvey. I still believe she was arguing with Beowulf, and he's the most likely suspect."

"What of it? He argues with all sorts of people. He argued with me, the jackanapes." His Lordship was still irritated by the monumental effrontery of the man, daring to come uninvited to his reception and then questioning him in that annoying way.

Mr. Eccleston rose from the sofa and began pacing in front of the fireplace. "Did you notice, Darvey, that both Beowulf and Miss Hanley have the same color hair?"

"Indeed, they do not." His Lordship's voice was sharp. "Beowulf's is an ugly rusty shade, whereas Elizabeth's hair is burnished, like fall leaves or . . ." His poetic inventiveness left him. "I don't know what, but I think perhaps you should go to bed, too, Eccleston. The late hour has addled your brain."

Mr. Eccleston's chin jutted out stubbornly. "You can't deny that their hair color is in the same family."

His Lordship gave his friend a look of exasperation. "That hardly proves that they are. You know, Eccleston, I am amazed by your primitive thinking. I suppose that if a black cat crossed your path and then your cow died, you would blame it on the cat."

"No, I wouldn't." Mr. Eccleston looked scornful. "I don't have a cow. And though I do not mean to be cruel, Justin, you do not have a whole manuscript, either. Someone who was here tonight took it."

His Lordship grimaced. "I cannot gainsay that."

Peter Eccleston gave him a sheepish grin. "I know it sounds as though I am fishing. Nevertheless, I still think there may be a connection between Lord Beowulf and Miss Hanley."

His Lordship shuddered. "How could you even attempt to compare them? She is so beautiful, and he . . . never mind. This conversation is stupid, and I'm more convinced than ever that your wits have gone abegging."

"Perhaps they have," Mr. Eccleston said amiably. "But consider this. Didn't Beowulf leave at the same time as old Cranley, and wasn't Cranley the one who recommended Miss Hanley to you? I think there might be something to think about there, don't you?"

Lord Darvey shifted his weight impatiently. "Indeed, I do not. You are still fishing, Peter."

"I suppose you may be right. Yet, I can't help having this niggling feeling . . ."

"And you call yourself a man of science? Next, you will

be consulting a fortune teller as to the whereabouts of my paper."

Mr. Eccleston clapped his friend on the shoulder. "All right. I will let it drop." Before Lord Darvey could get out more than a single sigh of relief, he added, "I just want to say, however, that it seems to me when it comes to Miss Hanley, you are the one who needs to worry about his wits."

"What do you mean?" His Lordship sounded offended.

Peter Eccleston looked earnestly into his friend's cold, grey eyes. "I mean, Justin, that from the first time you saw her, you seemed to cast aside all of your customary caution and overlook things that in someone else might give you pause. I am convinced that if you thought your research was questionable, you'd be ready to abandon it in a minute. And yet, when it comes to Miss Hanley, you ignore anything that doesn't fit your preconceived notion of her. It is very strange."

"Don't be absurd! There is nothing to ignore, because she is exactly as she seems. For some freakish, unfathomable reason, you just don't care for her.

"No, don't accompany me." With icy mien, his Lordship strode from the room, leaving his friend behind.

Eight

An invitation came to the house from Lady Thea, the young woman whom David had met in Hyde Park. It invited Elizabeth, Lady Treadway, and Lord Darvey to a ball. Only Elizabeth, however, accepted, although she didn't want to. She did so because his Lordship insisted.

"Turn around slowly," he commanded her now as she stood waiting with her brother for the carriage that would take them to Hanover Square. Elizabeth made a self-conscious pirouette. She was dressed for Lady Thea's ball in a pale green gown that mimicked the color of her eyes. Her smooth white shoulders and the tops of her breasts showed comely above it. For a brief instant, passion flared in his Lordship's eyes. Then his lashes swept down in concealment.

"This is for you to wear tonight," he said, taking a flat box from a pocket in his coat. He glanced once again at the alabaster skin above her bodice. "Here, Hanley," he said gruffly, "why don't you fasten it for her? There is one other thing that I need to get." Brusquely, he walked away.

Opening the box, David revealed a string of perfect pink-tinged pearls. "Oh," gasped Elizabeth. "How beautiful. I cannot wear them."

"You must," said his Lordship, having returned unnoticed. "They were my mother's and have been lying about for ages being useless. I do not like useless things. Fasten them up, Hanley."

Elizabeth doubted that his Lordship's mother would have approved of a companion borrowing her necklace. Nor would his fiancée's mother, though she doubted that Miss Brimmer would care a fig. Nevertheless, one look at Lord Darvey's face told her she must not argue. "Thank you," she said as graciously as she could manage.

He handed her a corsage of pink rosebuds tied with shiny green ribbon. "This is from Eccleston. He said he especially wished you to have it."

Indeed, he had. Wanting desperately to get back in his Lordship's good graces, he would have done anything for Elizabeth. Darvey had to stop him from offering her the Eccleston family emeralds.

Elizabeth's green eyes glistened with tears. "How can I thank you . . . thank you both? You are so good."

His Lordship cast a sidelong glance at her obviously restless brother. "You had best go along before Mr. Hanley loses all of his patience. I wish I, too, could be there, but I fear it is impossible. Please tender Lady Thea my regrets."

Up to that minute, despite his not being dressed in evening attire, Elizabeth had hoped that Lord Darvey still might attend the ball. Just this once, she wanted to dance with him.

She gave a tiny toss of her russet curls. One could not have everything, and look at all that she did have this night. With a jaunty smile, she took her twin's arm and left for the ball.

David was obviously nervous on the way to Hanover Square. "Suppose Lady Thea has no time for me, Liz? As hostess, she will be certain to be busy. Do you think she'll have saved a dance for me? Probably not," he answered his own question gloomily.

"David Hanley, stop that this minute. Lady Thea likes you; I am sure that she has saved you a dance."

His strong, narrow hands crushed hers. "Do you think so, that she likes me, I mean? I like her, Liz. I did from the very first minute I saw her. You probably do not think that is possible, but I assure you that it is."

"Yes, I think it is possible." Elizabeth freed her hands to give her brother an encouraging pat upon the arm. Her mind was not on what she was doing, however. She was remembering that first time she had seen Justin Darvey, his mouth twitching with suppressed mirth as he reached to catch Primrose's fly-away cage. She must store her memories carefully. Soon they would be all that she'd have of him.

Her brother peered from the carriage. "I think—yes, this is the house. It looks different at night." Almost tripping on the lowered steps, he got down from the carriage and then helped Elizabeth to descend.

Their hostess was towering over her parents at the door to the salon. She pumped the twins' hands. "How good to see you. Miss Hanley, you are in looks tonight."

She, herself, was garbed in a crimson jacquard tunic dress, and her long brown hair was caught up in a magnificent diamond-studded fillet. Although the current style did not quite suit her, she nevertheless managed to appear imposing.

The salon was a room of impressive size, lit by three huge crystal chandeliers which gave an attractive glow to the faces of the guests. The furniture, covered mostly in crimson brocade that matched the color of Lady Thea's gown, was lined up along the pale gold walls, leaving a large empty area for the dancers and those who wished to promenade.

"There is someone I want you to meet," said Lady Thea, leaving her parents to greet the guests so that she could shepherd Elizabeth and David across the floor. She led them to a pleasant-looking blond man of medium height who appeared to be about Lord Darvey's age. "Miss Hanley and

Mr. Hanley, you must be introduced to my cousin, Lord North."

Although his Lordship greeted the twins with the same degree of affability, it was apparent that his interest had been caught solely by Elizabeth. Following several minutes of general conversation, he asked her to stand up with him for the quadrille that was forming.

Lord North was an excellent dancer and a pleasant companion, having no strong opinions about anything but seeming to like all things equally well. Elizabeth enjoyed listening to his chatter as they strolled about the room after the dance ended.

Presumably, his Lordship continued to find her company agreeable, too. After securing her promise for the supper dance, he remained by her side much longer than mere good manners dictated.

They were just about to walk into the dining room, where a lavish collation had been laid out, when Lady Thea stopped them. "Go in with Mr. Hanley, North," she said peremptorily. "There is something I must say to Miss Hanley."

"I wanted you to know," she said after they'd left, "that you've made a conquest of my cousin. At his urging, I told him some things about you, including the information that you are a companion at present."

Elizabeth looked startled. "Did my brother tell you so?"

"Yes, what does it matter?" Lady Thea said impatiently. "What I'm attempting to say is that Lord North is taken with you. He would make a good husband, you know."

Elizabeth knew she should have felt flattered. Indeed, if she had met him before she'd come to care for Lord Darvey, she thought she might have been a little puffed up by his attentions. As it was, she experienced no more than a mild interest in him, which she was convinced would never increase. Whether she willed it or not, her feelings were all for Lord Darvey.

"Well?" Lady Thea demanded, putting her hands to her

hips in a most unladylike gesture. "You won't always be a companion, you know. Some day your brother will be established and things will be different for you . . . and everybody, don't you think?"

Her voice trailed off into a barely veiled plea for reassurance, but Elizabeth did not notice. Her heart in her eyes, she was watching Lord Darvey. Faultlessly attired in black pantaloons and a gilt-buttoned blue coat, he strode toward them across the polished parquet floor.

He bowed gracefully over both ladies' gloved hands. "I hope you will accept my apology for being late. I was unavoidably detained."

"Since you declined my invitation," Lady Thea replied tartly, "I can hardly consider you as late."

His Lordship's teeth sparkled in his tanned face. "That is good news. But don't let me delay you here at the door. May I escort you in to supper?"

Ignoring Elizabeth's joyful acceptance, Lady Thea said, "You may escort us, of course, but that is all. Both Miss Hanley and I are bespoken."

Lord Darvey gave Elizabeth a reproachful look that almost caused her to apologize. "Could . . . couldn't room be made at our table for his Lordship?" she heard herself beg Lady Thea.

"Certainly not," replied that redoubtable female. Taking Elizabeth's arm in a firm grip, she propelled her into the dining room.

Once settled between Lord North and her brother, Elizabeth gazed about the crowded room made noisy by laughter and the hum of numerous conversations. How very odd, she thought with an unconscious frown; she hadn't noticed before the number of attractive young women Lady Thea had invited that evening. Lord Darvey was seated between two of them—dark-haired, dark-eyed, hardened flirts, if the seasoned way they plied their fans was any indication. She was sure that it was.

She hoped they knew that Lord Darvey was engaged, she

thought righteously, remembering it herself for the first time that evening.

She tried not to glance at his Lordship after that, but her eyes continually strayed to his table despite her best intentions. It was a foolish thing to do since what she saw increasingly annoyed her. Did he have to have quite that good a time? She stared at him with a stony expression.

In between looks, she talked with Lord North, twitched her dimples at him, and laughed at all of his sallies, whether they merited it or not. In fact, one might have thought that she was enjoying herself quite as much as was Lord Darvey.

At last the interminable supper was over. Feeling grateful, Elizabeth prepared to rise from the table. "May I?" A deep, familiar voice prickled her ears, and her chair was practically jerked out from under her.

"Just a minute," said Lord North. "Is something wrong, Miss Hanley?"

Lord Darvey stared down his thin nose at him. "Of course, it is not," he said coldly. "Come, Elizabeth." Grasping her arm in his hard fingers, he returned her to the salon.

Almost as soon as they entered, they were approached by the Marquis of Clenmere to whom Elizabeth had promised the next dance. "We shall walk," said Lord Darvey, ignoring the Marquis, and marched her off toward the music room.

Without a glance for its white and gold walls hung with sketches by Rembrandt and Vermeer, he steered her to a silk settee and pulled forward a chair for himself. "You appeared to be keeping yourself amused at supper," he said in a censorious voice after they were seated. "Who was that man you were with? There was something about his face that I did not like."

Elizabeth decided she did not care for his Lordship's high-handed manner. Although she lived in his house and was acting as his great aunt's companion, she had no opinion of his involving himself in her affairs in that way.

"How is Miss Brimmer, your Lordship? I have not seen her much of late."

Lord Darvey stared at Elizabeth as though she had suddenly hoisted her skirts to show off her knees. "What does that have to say to the matter?" he replied in arctic accents. "You have not answered my question."

"Lord North!" snapped Elizabeth. "He is Lord North! He is Lady Thea's cousin and as respectable as she."

For answer, Lord Darvey snorted.

They were quarreling; that much was obvious. As to the reason, neither of them could have said.

"You should not take offense," his Lordship said stiffly, tugging at one of the gilt buttons on his coat. "I only want what is best for you. I was not certain that your brother could be relied upon to look after you, you see."

In fact, Elizabeth did not see, but suddenly it did not matter. Lord Darvey's long, well-shaped legs were so close that if he moved but a little they would touch her own; his nearness was intoxicating. What did she care if he disapproved of Lord North's looks? It was his Lordship's wonderful face that filled her daydreams.

"You needn't worry," she said, gently taking from his fingers the button he had twisted off. "Truly, Lord North's manners are as fine as one could wish for."

"Indeed? I believe he's formed a *tendre* for you. You must feel gratified."

How could he think it? There was only one person Elizabeth wished to have care for her, but her wish would never come true.

"I think I would like to leave now," she said with a brooding expression. "I must go and seek out my brother."

His Lordship stopped her by putting his hand around her wrist. "Why separate him so soon from his lady love? I shall take you home."

In the carriage, they sat tensely across from each other, and neither of them spoke. Then Lord Darvey said abruptly,

"I meant to ask you what your perfume is. It is not your usual scent."

"It is Miss in Her Teens," Elizabeth told him. "You bade Mr. Eccleston purchase it for me. Do you not remember?"

His Lordship shook his head. "I assure you that it must have been his idea. I prefer the one you usually wear that smells like the first roses of summer."

Elizabeth had not imagined he even knew that she wore perfume let alone was aware that she had changed it. He must pay her more heed than she had suspected, she thought with some confusion. She did not know what to make of it.

Then she chided herself for her thoughts. Lord Darvey was a natural philosopher, used to observing the smallest details. It meant nothing that he noticed insignificant things about her.

After that conversation, both again retreated into their own thoughts, and except for a rather awkward leave-taking when they were once again in his Lordship's town house, they had hardly anything further to say to each other. With an artificially bright smile, Elizabeth made her curtsy to Lord Darvey. Then she took her candle and made her way alone up the stairs.

She entered her apartment with a feeling of gratitude for having reached a safe harbor. It had turned out to be rather a dreadful evening, she thought, as she moodily scrubbed at the places where she had dabbed the Miss in her Teens. On a whim, she replaced it with the perfume she usually wore made from attar of roses.

She had just gotten into bed and pulled up her blue counterpane when she thought she heard someone outside her door. For a moment, compounded half of panic and half of hope, she thought it might be his Lordship come to talk to her again. Then she dismissed the idea. He would not do anything so foolishly compromising. She must have imagined the sound.

In fact, it was his Lordship standing in the hall with his hand raised to knock for admittance. Stymied by indecision, he left it suspended in the air. What would he say to Elizabeth if she answered his knock? He did not know, although he knew what he wanted to do. He wanted to sweep her into his arms and kiss her, first her mouth, then her eyes, then the sweet white skin of her shoulders and breasts. As he thought this, his nostrils flared. He could swear that he smelled roses.

He continued to hesitate. Then he dropped his hand. What was he doing standing like a heated-up stallion outside Miss Hanley's door? "Go to bed, Darvey," he told himself. "Dream of Fidelia Brimmer, if you can manage this time to remember what she looks like."

Inside the room, Elizabeth's rigidly held shoulders relaxed. She must have been imagining things, she thought. No one had knocked after all. "Go to bed, you foolish thing," she scolded herself. "And do not dream of Lord Darvey."

The first thing upon arising the next morning, Elizabeth read the letter from her uncle which David had slipped into her hand the day before. As usual, it was filled with insults and demands for more information. Not in the best of moods to begin with, she felt her temper flare. So, he wanted information, did he?

Taking a pen from her standish, she wrote: "I am glad that you asked about Lord Darvey's new paper because it is new, indeed. Now he believes that *small* skulls are a mark of intellectual superiority. His reasoning, as I understand it, is this: In a small skull, the brain is compacted, or, as he likes to say, reduced to its essence. Therefore, it is stronger, or more intelligent, than a brain that, by having more room to expand, is more diffuse. That is the gist of it. I hope I have put his idea clearly."

She wondered what her uncle would make of the nonsense she had written. She wished she could be there to see his response—though she would undoubtedly be cast out upon the road for her trickery when she finally returned home. Despite that thought, she could not help but chuckle as she put down her pen. Then she went off to find her brother, to give him the letter and wish him farewell.

The rest of the morning she spent with Lady Treadway, amusing her with Irish nonsense verse until it was time for her Ladyship's nap. After tucking the old lady in and kissing her, Elizabeth started for the laboratory with some trepidation. She and Lord Darvey had not parted amicably after all.

"I was just about to send a footman to fetch you," his Lordship said coolly when she entered the room. "You have a guest awaiting you in the library, Miss Hanley." He looked at her simple blue paisley dress and wool shawl and then shrugged. "You will not want to keep him waiting."

It was hardly a surprise, of course, when her caller turned out to be Lord North; from his attentions the previous evening, she had assumed that he might pay her a visit. Still, nothing could have prepared her for what he had to say.

Lord North seated himself in a velvet chair across from the one she chose. While she tried not to fidget, he arranged the tails of his nut brown coat and then fixed her with a sincere gaze. "I spoke at some length with my cousin, Lady Thea, last night; it was about you. She said that due to an unfortunate circumstance you are employed here as a companion."

Observing her heightened color, he said, "Are you embarrassed? Please do not be. Myself, I am delighted." At her look of surprise, he stopped speaking to give her a hopeful grin. "I think you will not find it strange when I explain.

"The truth is, I am depending on it that your present situation will make you amenable to my proposition, Miss Hanley. Lest you be alarmed, let me assure you that it is an honorable one. I wish you to become my wife."

"Your Lordship, you astonish me," Elizabeth said without exaggeration. "Since you could not possibly have formed any strong feeling for me in the short time we have been acquainted, and—despite your disclaimer—given my inferior status at present, I cannot understand why you would want me to be your wife."

"If you'll allow me. . . ." Lord North folded one of Elizabeth's small, nervous hands into his. "I will not pitch you any gammon. I must marry quickly, or my grandfather promises to disinherit me. I do not want to go into it, unless you insist, but I have not been—that is, he has expressed unhappiness over my single state for several years."

"Indeed?" Elizabeth gently freed her hand. "Then I do not understand why you have decided to do something about the situation now."

Lord North laughed uneasily. "Oh, that is simple. Last week he told me that if I did not finally do the deed by April, he would certainly carry out his threat this time. He never set a date before, so you can appreciate why I feel a certain urgency at this point, can you not, especially since most young women . . . their mommas wouldn't . . . you understand my meaning, don't you?" Rather in the style of Fidelia Brimmer, he ended his remarks with a vague, unfocused smile.

"Indeed, I do." Elizabeth could not help but smile in return. "I'm afraid, however, that although you may have a good reason for proposing to me, I do not have any for accepting. Therefore, regretfully, I must refuse your offer."

Lord North gave a desperate tug at his cravat. "I beg you, Miss Hanley, do not do that. Or at least swear that you will give the matter some more thought. I have a great deal to offer, you know—or will if I am not disinherited. Just think, I could perhaps set your brother up on one of my grandfather's estates, which Lady Thea tells me is greatly to be desired. In addition, I promise to be very good to you and make you come to love me. As for me, I am near in love with you already. Please say yes."

Unconsciously, Elizabeth's hands began to twist the fringes of her shawl. There was no denying that Lord

North's offer was tempting. Certainly, it would solve some of her problems, and David's. Perhaps it was foolish of her to refuse. "You have given me much to think about," she said, dropping her hands to her sides. "Can you wait a few days for my answer?"

Lord North sighed. "I suppose I shall have to. I hope you will believe me, Miss Hanley, when I tell you that of all the women I have met, I am most at ease with you. Sometimes a person feels that way even after a very short acquaintance."

How true, thought Elizabeth, trying not to think longingly about Lord Darvey. She said, "I will give you my answer shortly."

After he left, she contemplated returning to the laboratory but decided to go to her room instead. She was not ready to face Lord Darvey. Still, she felt lonely. She missed working alongside of his Lordship. She missed gazing into his beloved face. How difficult it would be when she no longer had any hope of ever seeing him again.

It was more than an hour after she retired for the night that she gave up trying to sleep. Putting on her robe and slippers and taking up a candle, she made her way downstairs to the library where she had noticed a copy of *Pride and Prejudice* a few days before. If she could not sleep, perhaps she could at least distract herself for awhile.

Clutching her candle, Elizabeth searched the full shelves until she found the volume she wanted. Then she pulled a chair up to the fireplace, where a log fire still burned brightly. She might as well stay until the fire burned down, she thought, sinking into the chair's blue velvet depths.

The chapters of the book were quite short, and she was well into Chapter Four when a sudden draft made her look up. Lord Darvey, a glass of port in his hand, stood just inside the room's tall, paneled doors.

"I thought for a minute that you were an apparition, but since I am a man of science and have reservations about such things. . . ." Not bothering to finish his sentence, he moved in her direction.

The light coming from the fireplace accentuated the strong bones of Lord Darvey's face and burnished his dark, curly hair. He was so handsome, thought Elizabeth, and so unobtainable that he might as well have been an apparition himself.

"No, do not stand up." Reaching her, he set down his glass, then put his hand upon her shoulder. "What is that you are reading? Oh, yes, I remember when the bookseller sent it. I do not have time for that sort of thing myself. You must tell me what it is about."

Managing to slip under his hand, Elizabeth put down the book and stood. "I think it is about love and marriage," she said in a low voice. "I like it very much."

"Is that so? Tell me, how did your visit go with your suitor this morning?"

Elizabeth's eyes searched his face. Despite the polite smile it sported, it seemed strained and distant. She felt as though he had erected a wall to keep her away. "He is not my. . . ." She brushed a suddenly shaking hand through her russet curls. "Perhaps he is. He has asked me to marry him."

"Marry him?" His Lordship laughed harshly. "Isn't that rather sudden?"

Elizabeth shrugged her slender shoulders. "One might say that. However, he must be excused because he is in a hurry. If he does not marry soon, he will forfeit his inheritance."

"It is absurd." Lord Darvey's lips thinned with anger. "He only wants to use you for his own ends. I will not allow it."

Elizabeth said gently, "I am afraid it is not up to you, my lord. I am of age, but if I were to ask for anyone's approval, it would be my brother's."

"Oh, yes. I suppose I forgot. However, I'm sure he must say no."

"Must he? Why is that? Do you know something terrible about Lord North?"

His Lordship looked surprised. "Why, no. In fact, I don't know anything about him at all. Nor do you; there's the rub. You should at least consider carefully before you come to a decision, Elizabeth. Unless, of course, you feel that you are already beginning to care for him?"

"No." She shook her head dispiritedly. "No, I do not especially care for him."

Lord Darvey knew that he should not be trying to dissuade Elizabeth from the match. Certainly, he did not have anything to offer her himself. Still, he could not seem to stop himself, because the thought of her marrying North was repugnant to him.

He enfolded her hands firmly between his. "Listen to me, then. I have discovered. . . . I think it would be a mistake for someone like you to marry without love. Do not marry him if you cannot care. We can work something out; I am sure that we can."

"I do not understand what you are saying." Elizabeth looked at his Lordship, her green eyes suddenly hopeful. "Have you some other plan for me, I mean for David and me?"

Lord Darvey took the place she had vacated on the couch and gestured to her to sit down beside him. "No, I fear I do not, but there must be something. The important thing is not to be hasty."

"I promise I won't be," she said.

Darvey felt pleased, although he did not know what he had accomplished. In fact, he admitted to himself fatalistically, when it came to his great aunt's companion, not knowing what he was doing seemed to have become his usual condition.

The two of them sat looking at each other in the warm glow of the fire's light. Ignoring the warning voice in his head, Darvey put his arm about her. "Elizabeth?"

"Yes, my lord?" Her cat's eyes were drowsy, and there was an unmistakable note of expectancy in her voice.

Reason fought with desire in his Lordship's breast and, for the moment, at least, won. "Nothing. It is nothing. I mean, I am sharp-set. Come, accompany me to the kitchen so that we can find something to eat."

Elizabeth contended with a strong feeling of disappointment, as though she had been promised something wonderful only to have it snatched away.

As for Lord Darvey, it was clear to him that he still did not have himself completely under control. He should have sent her off just then, and had meant to, but unwilling at the last minute to part from her, he had made up the excuse of being hungry.

No, in fact, he had quite a dreadful hunger, but it was not for bread and cheese. Maybe he would overcome the voice of reason that insisted upon trying to dissuade him and attempt to gain what he wanted this night.

"Come," he repeated. Taking her by the hand, he led her from the room.

In the kitchen the fire was banked in the big brick hearth that dominated one wall, so that most of the cavernous space was in darkness. "Wait here," Lord Darvey ordered, leaving Elizabeth at the entrance to the room. He walked over to stoke the fire to life, his Spanish leather pumps making sharp, crackling sounds on the bare planked floor.

"You may come in now," he said after a few minutes, "and sit at the table. Tonight I shall wait upon you."

Elizabeth obediently began to walk to where he had pointed but halted before she got very far. Something strange was occurring. There was an unpleasant sensation of movement under the thin soles of her slippers, as though parts of the floor were alive.

She peered around nervously, but there was nothing to be seen in the darkness at her feet. She took a few more tentative steps and stopped.

She was closer to the table now, where his Lordship had

placed several lit rushes. By their dim light, she looked down at the floor to see what might be there. All about her were fat, black objects, objects that moved. Unable to stop herself, she screamed.

"What is it?" Lord Darvey came at once to her side. Instead of answering, Elizabeth leaped upon his shoes. Her little slippers clung to them like limpets.

"Oh . . . ugh. It is beetles. Great, black, shiny ones. I think some are stuck to my slippers." She plastered her body against his. "I do not think I can bear it, my lord."

Lord Darvey bit his lower lip several times, then he started to laugh. "I am sorry," he apologized as he felt her poker up, "but I can't seem to help myself. There's just something ludicrous about your fearing a common cellar beetle when you never turned a hair over my skulls."

"I can't help it, either," Elizabeth mumbled into his chest. "What's more, if you don't remove me from this room at once, I believe that I shall cry."

"Don't do that," Lord Darvey said hastily before planting a light kiss upon her hair. Then he pried her loose to cradle her in his arms. Accompanying his movements with soft, soothing sounds, he carried her up the back stairs and to her suite of rooms.

Elizabeth looked down shyly at him from the blue and white sofa as he bent to remove her offending slippers. "Oh, my lord, I am sorry to be such a fool, but I just can't abide beetles; they give me the cold creeps."

Lord Darvey's long fingers spread caressingly across her feet and ankles. Then they stopped, and he slowly straightened. "It seems there are things I cannot abide, either, although I swear that I have tried." With the sigh of a man resigning himself to fate, he seated himself beside her and turned her so that she faced him.

Elizabeth gazed apprehensively into his smoky grey eyes. They looked lazy, almost sleepy, except for something hot sparking in their depths. It made her shiver.

"My lord," she stammered, "I don't believe—I'm

afraid. . . ." Her voice trailed off. It was difficult to think clearly when she was fighting to rein in her own impetuous desires. But rein them in she must, for both their sakes. Whatever madness was causing his Lordship to abandon his customary caution, he would not be glad of it later when he was his usual rational self again.

"I appeal to your reason," she said gravely, confident that she had hit upon the right argument. "You must leave me now."

One hard hand moved to Elizabeth's chin and tilted it so that her ripe mouth was directly below his. "I am tired of reason." Lord Darvey's husky tone was impatient. "All I know is that I mean to kiss you and love you till you cry mercy, Elizabeth. As to my feelings, I'll examine them some other time."

Nine

LORD DARVEY'S WARM lips moved urgently over Elizabeth's, cajoling and demanding. What could she do? Her few defenses crumbled under the assault. Opening the sweetness of her mouth to him, she let him plunder it as he would.

No pirate could have gathered treasure more ably. In a minute, her senses were reeling and she could not think. Following blind instinct, she touched the jet curls that lay along the sides of his face, softening its strong lines. Then her fingers probed the tanned skin beneath.

With a groan, his Lordship pulled down Elizabeth's small, white hands and kissed them. Still holding them, he leaned forward to slide his tongue over her upper lip from one moist edge to the other. His mouth moved to the throbbing artery in her neck and stopped just above the swell of her breasts.

By now, Elizabeth was lying on one hip, her back against the upright sofa cushions. Lord Darvey lay beside her so that she felt his body burn along hers from her waist to the ends of her toes.

What was happening was not right, and it was not clever. But—oh, glory—it was heaven, and she did not want it to stop.

Lord Darvey did not disappoint her. Cupping his hands

beneath her breasts, he lifted the satiny flesh. Then he bent his head to taste the warm, sweet valley between; it smelled intoxicatingly of roses.

Heat spread from the spot where his lips rested, down Elizabeth's belly, to the place between her legs. And, suddenly, she felt ashamed. She should not be having such sensations; they were wrong. And what she was doing, or at least allowing to be done to her, was just as bad, if not worse. She was a wanton, for very certain.

"My lord. . . ." Even to her, her voice sounded as though it was coming from a great distance. "My lord, I beg you, please stop."

Seeming lost in his longing to possess her, Justin Darvey did not respond to her plea. "I beg you," she repeated huskily, and knew she was pleading as much with herself as with him to control the feelings he had set loose.

This time, though with obvious reluctance, Lord Darvey drew back from her and sat up. "Little one, have I frightened you?" His low voice was ragged. "I am sorry for it if I have."

She believed him. Nevertheless, from the hungry look on his face, she was not certain that she could trust him—or herself. Before he might decide to reach for her again, and she allow it, Elizabeth stumbled to her feet. She went to stand beside Primrose's cage as though in need of the tiny bird's moral support. Indeed, despite the fact that she had called a halt to their love-making, her morals needed support.

His Lordship used this time to study her. With her tousled auburn curls and swollen, kissed lips, she looked entirely bewitching. "Damn Fidelia!" He swore under his breath. He could wish her to Hades.

Hardly aware of what he was doing, he adjusted his cravat several times, then donned his coat, which he had uncharacteristically thrown to the floor some time before. Making no attempt to draw nearer to Elizabeth, he sighed and said, "You are right. This is madness, and it must end."

She should have been pleased that he agreed with her, but, paradoxically, Elizabeth felt only despair. "I shall leave in the morning," she said, trying to keep her voice steady. "You need not worry, my lord, about any future entanglement. I will not be here."

Elizabeth was used to seeing Lord Darvey's autocratic features made mellow by his normally tolerant nature. This time, such was not the case. Anger gave him a dangerously imperious look. "Indeed, you will not leave," he growled at her. "I shall not permit it. You will stay here, Elizabeth—at least, that is, until I find what's to be done with you."

With unconscious grace, he moved across the space that separated them and imprisoned her slender wrists in his hands. "Promise me that you will obey me in this. I want your word on it."

With his stubbornly thrust-out chin, he looked as if he might not budge from her room forever if she didn't do as he ordered. "You have it," she said softly, eager now above all things to mollify him.

"Good girl." He accompanied the words with an approving smile. "Now you must promise me something else as well. You must swear to try not to be distressed about what took place here between us tonight. It was only natural for you to turn to me for solace after the fright you received. What was wrong was my taking advantage of your weakened state."

"Oh, no," she protested, almost throwing herself into his arms once more. "You must not say that. At least, it was my fault as much as it was yours."

Lord Darvey's grin made him seem more like the man she was used to. "If it makes you feel better to share the guilt, so be it."

Elizabeth's answering smile deepened the little dimples at the edges of her lips. This charming display nearly caused his Lordship to groan aloud.

He was greatly tempted to tell her that he would marry her if he were free, but he forced himself to hold back the words. It was the unvarnished truth, but what was the use of saying it? He was not free; therefore his wishes meant nothing.

No gentleman cried off from an engagement; it simply was not done. Even if he could bring himself to it, it would be a poor sort of a solution. Not only would he be branded a cad and shunned by his fellows at the Royal Society, but also he'd probably have to accept Barton Brimmer's challenge to fight a duel. Then he'd have to leave the country and. . . . Oh, what was the use? He was caught unless he could think of some way to make Fidelia want to break it off herself. What that would be, considering that her mother appeared to desire the engagement strongly, he could not begin to imagine.

"I wish to make you two promises." Lord Darvey reined in his thoughts to address Elizabeth. "One is that I give you my word that this will not happen again. The other is that I will do what I can to help your brother and you—unless, that is, you decide after all to marry North, in which case you will not need anyone's help."

Why had he brought up that possibility again? Hadn't they already discussed it, and hadn't his Lordship begged her not to take that step? Elizabeth couldn't help thinking that despite his words, he must want to be rid of her. And who could blame him? It would be the easiest solution of all, for him if not for her.

Still, she would do nothing until after he read his paper. He would need her assistance till then. Besides, how could she bear to leave him before it? How could she not be there in April to share his triumph and his joy? It did not bear thinking on.

Yet she needed to stay out of his clutches. Good intentions could fail. Didn't she know that from her own experience? She must be determined for them both.

"My lord, you must forgive me." She forced herself to yawn. "I find I am most dreadfully tired. The excitement. . . ." Elizabeth broke off and blushed scarlet.

"I mean the beetles and the . . . uh . . . beetles. I must bid you good night, my lord."

Joining her at the door, his Lordship leaned forward as though to give her a parting kiss, but Elizabeth neatly stepped to one side. "Good night," he said instead, his grey eyes rueful as he scrutinized her partly averted face. "Sleep well, Elizabeth. I am counting on your help in the morning, you know. I could not finish my paper without you."

Greatly to her surprise, she did sleep well. Perhaps it was that having decided on a course of action, one, moreover, that she need follow only until the spring lecture, she felt relieved of the burden of making decisions. Her way was charted.

Still, the next morning, as she prepared to go to him while Lady Treadway took her nap, the remembrance of their intimacy the previous night made her dread facing him. Even with her feather duster clutched to her bosom like a shield, Elizabeth needed all her courage to walk into his Lordship's laboratory.

Once inside the sparsely furnished room, however, she felt her nervousness diminish when she saw that they were not to be alone. Mrs. Brimmer and Miss Brimmer were with his Lordship, the two women standing well away from the long worktable with its collection of skulls. Ordinarily, of course, Elizabeth would have disliked seeing the Brimmers, but this time, if not delighted, she was at least relieved.

"Oh, it's you." Mrs. Brimmer peered out from her purple velvet bonnet with a scowl. "Cannot you see that we are talking? You must come back later, after Miss Brimmer and I are gone."

The blondhaired young woman focused her agreeable, vacant smile upon Elizabeth. Unlike the latter, who, in an unconscious effort to hide, had donned a severe black round gown, she was dressed in the height of fashion in a yellow lutestring day dress and a spencer and kid slippers of moss green. She looked as fresh and pretty as a daffodil, Elizabeth thought gloomily. Perhaps his Lordship had some affection for her after all.

If so, he was concealing the fact admirably, for he seemed to be more annoyed than pleased by the ladies' presence. For Elizabeth, however, there was not even that much emotion in evidence. His thick, dark lashes sweeping down to conceal the expression in his eyes, he gave her the merest suggestion of a smile.

Oh, dear. She had neither expected nor wanted passion this morning, but to be greeted as though she were a mere acquaintance could hardly make her happy. "Excuse me," she said. "I shall come back later."

"No, don't go." Lord Darvey's lashes swept up, and his eyes took on a humorously pleading look. "As you are aware, the ladies do not care for my laboratory. Be so kind as to escort them to the library, where I will join you all after awhile."

Elizabeth was confused. Did he mean that she was to stay with the Brimmers? It seemed unlikely, but he had said *all*. Resigning herself to an unpleasant wait, she led the other women through the double doors into the library.

Although a fire was blazing in the grate, the room had not yet been tidied; the copy of *Pride and Prejudice* she had been reading the night before still lay where she had placed it. Blushing, she slipped it back into its place on the shelf.

Miss Brimmer strolled over to where Elizabeth was standing. "His Lordship was wrong, you know," she said sweetly. "It is not the laboratory I mind. It is the skulls. I am not like you, Miss Hanley, so no matter how I try I cannot seem to care for them."

Mrs. Brimmer snorted. "Of course, you are not like her, my darling. That goes without saying. As for the skulls, as I've told you and told you, you must not fret yourself about them. After awhile, Darvey will grow tired of them and give them up. Then we will put them in the attic—and take down all of the things we want." She ended her remarks with a spiteful look at Elizabeth.

"I don't know, Mama." Miss Brimmer smiled vaguely at her mother. "His Lordship seems excessively attached to them."

Mrs. Brimmer came to stand on the other side of her daughter, away from Elizabeth. "And what does that signify? Hasn't your brother been attached to things? Don't you remember the snuff boxes I mentioned before? Now he doesn't care for them even a little. Listen to your mother; men are fickle. It's one thing today and another tomorrow."

Looking at Miss Brimmer's newly optimistic expression, Elizabeth grimaced. If these women thought that his Lordship would give up his specimens for snuff boxes or some other frippery thing, like that disgusting Mr. Brimmer, they did not know him at all. Dear, wonderful Lord Darvey. He deserved better than the Brimmers. How sad that he was not going to get better.

Elizabeth was about to make an excuse so that she could escape their presence, even if his Lordship had meant for her to stay. However, she was prevented from doing so when the door from the outside hall opened and Hemmings announced Lady Palmer, Lady Thea, and Lord North. The latter she observed with some dismay. He was not to have returned so soon. She hoped he had not come to importune her once more.

Leaving the other two behind, Lady Thea walked rapidly across the polished, uncarpeted floor to reach Elizabeth's side. "My dear Miss Hanley, I trust we are not intruding. I could not wait to see you again."

Mrs. Brimmer's critical eye went over the interloper, no doubt cataloguing the obviously expensive red walking dress and black beaver hat adorned with red tassels and plumes. Elizabeth noticed that although her expression of dislike did not lessen, her air of hauteur did.

"I did not know that Miss Hanley had any friends," Miss Brimmer said cheerfully to Lady Thea upon being introduced to the three newcomers. "How pleasant for her that she does. Of course, I have my mother, and you have yours."

Lady Thea put her large hand to her mouth. "Never tell me this fool is Darvey's fiancée," she muttered behind it. "How did he ever get entrapped by her?"

"Let me order some refreshments," Elizabeth said for answer, attempting not to laugh. "I shall not be more than a minute."

When she returned to the room, followed by a maid with a laden tray, it was more like thirty minutes that she had been gone. Miss Brimmer was now talking to Lord North, who had a commiserating smile fixed on his lips, while Mrs. Brimmer stood nearby, nodding her head. The topic of conversation was Lord Darvey's skulls.

"There is little that I object to," Miss Brimmer said without exaggeration. "However, try as I might, I cannot seem to find any affection in myself for them."

"As though you could." Lord North agreed with her. "I cannot understand how Miss Hanley can bear to look at them."

Mrs. Brimmer snorted. "Oh, her."

"Yes, indeed. I quite agree." Miss Brimmer accompanied this statement with a toss of her soft blond curls.

As if suddenly coming to life, Lady Palmer rushed from the corner where she'd been cowering to reach Elizabeth's side. Her small feet almost slid on the bare wooden floor in her haste. "Dear, dear Miss Hanley," she said in a terrified voice, "I'm so pleased that you've come back. Now you can tell Mrs. Brimmer that I do not have any influence with Lord Darvey. She appears to think that I have, you know."

Elizabeth glanced quickly at each of the inhabitants of the room. It was her opinion that the whole lot of them belonged in Bedlam, except, perhaps, Lady Thea, and Elizabeth wasn't totally certain about her. What struck her as especially bizarre was that they were come together in Lord Darvey's house. He was such a sane, rational man—

most of the time. Remembering some of his behavior on the previous night, she blushed.

Forcing herself to pay attention to the agitated woman before her, she said, "I fear that I do not understand, Lady Palmer."

"It is perfectly simple," Lady Thea said in her brusque, direct way. "This—Mrs. Brimmer thinks Lord Darvey should give a ball, but she wants my mother to request it of him, I suppose because he had turned her down in the past."

"That is exactly right," Mrs. Brimmer said sourly.

Lady Palmer wrapped her thin arms tightly about herself as though endeavoring to keep some ravening beast from her meager breast. "You see," she whispered helplessly.

Before Elizabeth could think of a response, the door leading from the laboratory opened and Lord Darvey walked in, closely followed by Mr. Eccleston and a swaddled Lady Treadway in her chair. When his Lordship saw that the library's occupants had multiplied from three to six, he immediately changed his mind about being there and attempted to return to his laboratory. Unfortunately, his great aunt's chair blocked his way.

Opening his hands in a gesture of defeat, his Lordship turned again to face them. "How nice," he said coldly, at the same time looking askance at Elizabeth, as though she could have kept the lot of them away if she had but tried.

"Mrs. Brimmer was just talking about your giving a ball," Lady Thea, not one to waste words, addressed Lord Darvey with a mischievous light in her brown eyes. "It's to be in April, I believe. Isn't that right?"

"A ball!" boomed Lady Treadway. "Why not a masquerade? That's the very thing." She pointed at Mrs. Brimmer. "I'll come dressed as Bathsheba, and you can be the Abbess of Crewe. *There once was an Abbess of Crewe, who found a large . . .*"

Elizabeth popped a peppermint into Lady Treadway's mouth. Then she looked toward his Lordship, waiting for him to give them all a sharp set-down. To her surprise, however, he gazed with indifference around the group and then said, "Why not? Not a masquerade, of course, but I think we could have a ball."

"Why not?" Mrs. Brimmer asked indignantly, as though she had not recently been prodding Lady Palmer to obtain his Lordship's assent to that very thing. "I can't think how many times I've asked you in the past, and you've always said no. I do not understand why you're being so amenable now."

"Do you not?" His Lordship shrugged his strong shoulders inside his beautifully tailored green riding coat. "Perhaps I want to celebrate the reading of my paper, for it is directly after that event that I think we should have the ball. Perhaps I want to mark the end of things and a new beginning. I am not naturally a contemplative man; I do not know for certain."

Despite his laconic manner, Elizabeth sensed the presence in him of forces that strove against each other. She wondered uneasily whether that strife had to do with her and what the outcome would be.

If she was involved in his thoughts, she could not tell, for his Lordship barely looked at her after that. For awhile she hovered on the outside of the group, now animatedly discussing plans for the ball. Feeling distinctly *de trop*, she began to edge toward the door.

"Wait." Lord North hurried over to join her. "I came here specifically to talk to you again. Is there somewhere private we can go for a little chat?"

Lord Darvey took a step in their direction, a hard look on his face. Then, as though recalling something, he stopped and lifted his hands in a resigned gesture.

Mrs. Brimmer, however, was not subject to such self-inhibiting behavior. Her not quite inaudible mutterings about companions, impropriety, and one's place had rippled the surface of the others' conversations all along, but now she raised her voice. "I never heard the like."

"Use the salon," Lord Darvey said. "You can be quite private there."

A fire was burning brightly in one of the salon's two white marble fireplaces. The scent of its logs mingled with the smells of beeswax and lemon, but neither sight nor scent made an impression on Elizabeth. Nervous anticipation made her oblivious to her surroundings.

"My dear Miss Hanley," said Lord North, seating himself beside her on one of the elegant pale green sofas, "although I know I promised not to visit you for a few days, I found that I could not stay away. There is so little time. That is, I hope you have been thinking kindly of me and have reconsidered my suit. You know that your acceptance would make me the happiest man in the world, not to mention my grandfather and my cousin, Lady Thea. Please say yes."

Although she felt no urge to accept his suit in order to gratify all of his relatives, still, she wished she could give him the answer he wanted. If it had not been for the memory of Lord Darvey's kisses upon her willing lips, perhaps she might have done so. Undoubtedly, it would have been the sensible thing. Now, though, she knew absolutely that she could not marry Lord North. After her intimate encounter with Lord Darvey the previous night, the thought of being held and kissed and caressed by another man made her shudder.

But how was she to impart the news to Lord North? He had honored her with his proposal, and he was obviously a good, decent man. More than anything, she did not want to hurt him.

Choosing her words with care, she said, "Lord North, I cannot thank you enough for the honor you have done me, and I would very much like to say yes. I fear, however, that I cannot. You must not think that I do not admire and like you," she went on quickly as he started to interrupt her, "for, indeed, I do. In fact, that is one reason why I must refuse you."

"What?" Lord North looked confused. "I don't follow your line of reasoning."

"Oh, don't you see? If nothing else, it would be unfair in me to wed you, because I know that I can never love you."

Lord North grabbed her hand. "Is that all? You mustn't give it another thought. Nobody I know loves the person he gets leg-shackled to, at least at first. Why, it wouldn't be good ton if he did."

What could she say to dissuade him? The poor man! Elizabeth was torn by guilt and regret.

Pulling her hand away, she rose to put a little distance between them. As much as she loathed what she meant to do, there was nothing for it but to make a clean break. "My lord, my mind is made up, and nothing you say will change it. I cannot marry you."

At his groan, she almost sat down beside him again in order to offer him comfort. Only fear that he would mistake her kindness for a change of heart stopped her. "You will get over your disappointment," she said softly, "and you will find someone better than I. I know it."

"Do you?" Lord North's blue eyes suddenly looked hopeful. "How do you know it? Do you have someone else to recommend? I would be forever grateful to you, Miss Hanley, if you do."

So much for poor Lord North's sensibilities. Elizabeth did not know whether to laugh or—to laugh. She admitted to herself, though, that her feelings were just a wee bit hurt. Despite being aware that he could not truly have formed any deep affection for her, she had expected him to care about her refusal for more than a minute altogether.

"Well?" Lord North entreated her. "I'm waiting to hear the fair one's name."

"Fidelia Brimmer."

"Who? Do you mean that young woman I was talking with awhile ago in Lord Darvey's library? I somehow thought that she was Darvey's fiancée." He looked at her with surprise.

Elizabeth was as surprised as he. She hadn't had any idea that she was going to say Miss Brimmer's name until she heard herself pronounce it. She must have said it out of pique. "I was jesting," she told him weakly.

"Well, really!" This time it was very obvious that Lord North was nursing hurt feelings. His fair skin mottled with emotion, he quickly maneuvered around her and headed for the French doors that led to the garden as though he could not get away from her fast enough. "Don't bother to show me out," he said, very stiffly on his stiffs. "I'll find my own way. Good-bye, Miss Hanley, for I do not suppose that I shall see you again."

The taut line of Elizabeth's pretty mouth showed her distress. She still felt sorry for Lord North, despite the shallowness of his feeling for her. At the same time, she worried about what he would tell Lady Thea. She hoped the latter would not turn against David. "It's all my fault," she muttered in vague, indiscriminate guilt. "Everything."

Sighing unhappily, she left the room, to wander back into the laboratory. Unlike Miss Brimmer, for her it was a refuge, and she felt her mood lighten just because she was there. She stopped at Lord Darvey's worktable and gave one of the skulls an affectionate tap with the handle of her feather duster.

A few steps to her left, rows of shelves covered the wall. Without really thinking about what she was doing, Elizabeth began to dust the brass containers and other equipment that filled them.

She was just bending her knees to reach the containers nearest the floor when she heard a man's voice say, "Boo!" Startled, she flung out her hands, releasing the duster which landed atop the skull she had recently tapped. With the feathers covering its bald pate, it looked very frivolous, and Elizabeth almost laughed.

Being alone with Mr. Barton Brimmer, however—for that was the gentleman who had startled her—was not precisely a matter for mirth. It was not that Elizabeth feared him but that she simply could not care for the man. She had no desire to be in his presence, especially when there was no one else about to distract him.

Mr. Brimmer, fortunately, was not much inclined to visit his future brother-in-law, but she had seen him a time or two since he had felt her bottom. Except for a sly wink now and again, he always ignored her. A companion, after all, was beneath his touch—at least theoretically.

She noted that he looked somewhat rumpled, as though having just returned from a night of revelry. Indeed, when he came closer, she detected what seemed to be wine stains on his garments.

For his part, he seemed quite pleased to see her. He grinned, making his plump face look like a pumpkin, and he smoothed his blond locks as though to draw her attention to his attractions.

"Pray, excuse me," said Elizabeth, not at all attracted. "I was just leaving."

"What, so soon? Don't go." Mr. Brimmer's tone was wheedling. "It's been a long time since we've been together like this, hasn't it?" He bent forward to push in the tip of her nose. "I hope you didn't think I had forgotten you. Have you missed me?"

Had she missed being struck down by plague? Elizabeth was hard put not to reply thus to him or to slap his smirking countenance. If he had not been the brother of Lord Darvey's fiancée, indeed she might have done both.

"I think I hear Lord Darvey and Mr. Eccleston," she lied. "I shall just go out to see if they need anything."

Mr. Brimmer grinned like a chessy cat. "You needn't bother. They have gone to my house to look at some enameled boxes. For some reason, my mother was dead set on them seeing the things. At least she wanted Lord Darvey to see them." The grin changed to a leer worthy of the villain in a Cheltenham tragedy. "Which means that you and I are alone, my dear, and that you are at my mercy."

"You are mistaken if you believe that I am without

protection, sir," said Elizabeth, her green eyes contemptuous. "I have a brother who would be only too happy to impale you on his sword if I asked him to."

At this graphically drawn threat, Mr. Brimmer backed away from Elizabeth, although he continued to eye her audaciously. "I don't think he'd care to do that," he challenged from a safer place near one of the windows. "From what my sister tells me, he is wooing a titled lady. I doubt that her parents would approve if he created a scandal."

Probably not, thought Elizabeth, but certainly, if she read that lady aright, Lady Thea would. Elizabeth could imagine her standing by and cheering. Still, Mr. Brimmer had given her food for thought.

"Why do you not return home?" Now it was her turn to wheedle. "I can see that you are tired. In fact—in fact, you look rather ill. Are you sure that you are feeling quite the thing?"

Mr. Brimmer looked at her suspiciously. "What are you talking about? I am not ill. I'm not even tired, though I haven't been to bed yet. Are you trying to put a spell on me to make me sick?"

Would that she could. But, alas, she had no such powers. All she could do was go on as she had been doing in the hope that it would have an effect on him.

"I still say that you don't look well. There's been a whole rash of cases of the influenza lately. Are you sure that you don't have a fever?"

"Fever?" For a minute he looked uncertain. Then he laughed. "Yes, I have a fever. And it's because of you, you little imp." So saying, the unimpressionable Mr. Brimmer lunged at her.

Elizabeth did not take his athletic behavior too seriously. After all, Lord Darvey or any other inhabitant of the house could come walking into the laboratory at any moment. With a disgusted look, she grabbed the feather duster and pushed it into his face.

Mr. Brimmer sneezed violently several times, affording Elizabeth a chance to escape, which she was quick to take. Without a second's hesitation, she headed for the nearest door.

Before she could get there, however, he reached her side and grabbed hold of her. One of his hands went to her full breasts.

How dare he! Flushing with temper, Elizabeth struck her assailant on the arm.

"You devil." Mr. Brimmer grinned, as though they were playing a game. "I'll show you who's in charge here, vixen." So saying, he pushed one of his legs between hers in an effort to topple her to the floor.

Although still not precisely afraid, Elizabeth knew she had to put a stop to his actions, for he would not. As hard as she could, she shoved him against the shelves.

What happened after that seemed to progress very, very slowly. Elizabeth watched the shelves shake, then dislodge a shiny brass container. It fell upon Mr. Brimmer's head. At first, Mr. Brimmer merely looked surprised. Then his fat face went blank, and he dropped in an ungraceful heap to the floor.

With unnatural detachment, Elizabeth studied him as he lay sprawled at her feet. She noticed that he was very pale, making the yellowish freckles that covered his face stand out in sharp contrast.

Freckles? She did not remember Mr. Brimmer having freckles. In fact, she was certain he hadn't had any when he had come into the room. Her green eyes wide, she stared into the canister which had felled him. It was filled with mustard seed.

Dear me, she thought, trying to hold back hysterical laughter. Her uncle had been right. Mustard seed decidedly had its uses.

Ten

THE DAYS AND weeks following Elizabeth's rebuff of Lord North's and Mr. Brimmer's very different proposals were, on the surface at least, anticlimactic. Neither of the men returned, nor did she meet a single other importuning suitor or lecherous gentleman who might contrive to cut up her peace.

Which is not to say that she had any peace. How could she have, now that April was here?

Elizabeth had believed that she was prepared for its advent, but while she wasn't looking, it seemed, it arrived, along with the spring cyclamen and crocuses, and jolted her with its consequences. Foremost among them was that soon she must leave Grosvenor Square and never see Lord Darvey again.

Sometimes the sorrow caused by that thought brought such pain to her chest it felt as though her heart was literally breaking. At those times, Elizabeth would suck in her breath and stand rigid, in an effort to help herself get through the bad time.

Her other solution was to keep herself as busy as possible. Fortunately, what with carrying out her duties to Lady Treadway, assisting his Lordship to finish his experiments, and helping wherever she could with preparations for the impending ball, she found a great deal to which to devote herself. She also continued to send wildly imaginative letters to her uncle, each one expanding on the supposed topic of Lord Darvey's paper, so that David would have an excuse to come to town frequently and visit Lady Thea.

It would have surprised her to learn that just as Lord Darvey was the chief source of her unhappiness, so she was the source of his. Finding himself unable to do anything about his feelings for her, however, he kept his emotions to himself. He did not even tell Peter Eccleston—until that gentleman guessed what was the matter.

They were sitting together in the library at the big polished table ostensibly working on one of Mr. Eccleston's geometry problems. Try as he might, however, Lord Darvey could not put his mind to it. As usual, his thoughts were focused on Elizabeth.

The essence of those thoughts was that although he should do the sensible, logical thing and forget about her in a romantical way, he could not. Perhaps even a month before, he'd have denied the possibility, yet now he knew that when it came to his aunt's companion, logic had become irrelevant. He wanted her badly, devil take it. That was what was relevant.

Seeing his friend in such low spirits, Mr. Eccleston asked sympathetically, "Is it the paper? Are you afraid that you will not finish it in time?"

Lord Darvey rose. Then, keeping his eyes on the tips of his gleaming black Hessians, he began a slow perambulation about the room. "The paper is going well," he said. "Soon, in fact, I will start to make a fair copy of it, or Miss Hanley will."

He said her name in such a despairing voice that Mr. Eccleston, sprawled untidily in his seat, leaped up and pointed his finger at his friend. "That's it, isn't it, Justin? It's Miss Hanley. I mean, she's the reason for your being in the doldrums, isn't she?"

Staring coldly down at his friend, Lord Darvey started to

deny it, but then gave it up. "Yes, and yes, and what am I to do about it? I can't just jilt Fidelia Brimmer and run off with a young lady who's a member of my household."

For a moment, Mr. Eccleston looked thoughtful. Then he said, "No, I suppose you can't. But there must be something you can do."

Lord Darvey stopped before the large marble fireplace, to stare broodingly into the leaping flames. "I'm willing to listen if you can think of something feasible," he said, still keeping his gaze on the fire. "You're always full of suggestions. Give me a workable one if you have it, and you will see that I will jump to take it."

Mr. Eccleston tapped his brow with an ink-stained finger, as though attempting to dislodge a thought that had stuck there. "Let me see. Could you simply explain to Miss Brimmer . . . ? No, that would not do. Well, perhaps you could . . . No, I don't imagine that would work, either. I have it," he said, just as his Lordship seemed about to initiate an escape from the room. "Why don't you hint, delicately, of course, when Miss Hanley and Miss Brimmer are together, that you mean to make Miss Hanley your mistress? And then you could sort of leer at Miss Hanley and fondle her a bit. All executed in good taste, naturally; that goes without saying."

Lord Darvey's face took on an expression of disgust. "I shouldn't have asked you. When it comes to Miss Hanley, just about all you ever think of is my making her my mistress. You have a low mind, Eccleston."

"Is that so? Then, what, pray tell, were you thinking of making her?"

Red color rose under his Lordship's tanned skin, but he answered without hesitation, "Certainly not my mistress." Then he paused while Mr. Eccleston stared expectantly at him. "I suppose," he said in a low voice, "I was thinking of marrying her."

"No, really? Why?"

"What do you mean, why?" his Lordship snapped. "What sort of question is that?"

Mr. Eccleston's blue eyes gazed with unblinking sincerity into his friend's censorious grey ones. "I think it is a very good question. I'm trying to understand the basis for your conclusion that you want to marry your aunt's companion. Do you love her?"

"Love?" Lord Darvey repeated the word as though it were in some alien tongue.

Mr. Eccleston ran a finger along one of the stripes on his badly wrinkled waistcoat. "No need to look at me like that. I was only asking. Actually, I should have known that a rational man such as you would never succumb to one of Cupid's arrows."

His Lordship sighed, and his broad shoulders slacked inside his fawn-colored coat. "I'm afraid you're wrong, Eccleston. I'm not as rational as both of us once thought, nor am I immune to tender feelings. Do I love Miss Hanley?" His austerely handsome face softened. "Although I appear not to have considered the matter in that light until you asked, my friend, the answer would seem to be *yes*."

"Is that a fact?" Mr. Eccleston looked fascinated. "Upon my soul. I never thought I'd hear you say that. Well, then, we certainly will have to do something, won't we? Let me think."

Joining Lord Darvey in front of the fire, he bent his head toward an arrangement of hothouse lilies in the center of the mantel, as if searching out an answer among the waxy white petals. "I have it," he said, straightening with enthusiasm. "What you need is someone willing to take your place with Miss Brimmer upon the altar of Hymen."

"Are you offering yourself as a substitute?"

"Not I." Mr. Eccleston looked horrified. "Besides, she doesn't want me. Of course, she doesn't want you, either. Her mother does. What you need is to find someone her mother likes better."

"Don't be ridiculous. Her mother doesn't like anyone at all, so how could she like someone *better*?"

"That's true," Mr. Eccleston sighed. "I don't know what to tell you then, old boy. It looks as if you'll have to marry that smiling ninny after all."

Lord Darvey's usually inscrutable face subtly rearranged itself so that his features took on a hard, unyielding cast. "I shan't, you know, now that I've made up my mind. I'm going to think of something to dissuade her. I have to, Eccleston. There's no other choice." Turning neatly on his heel, he made for the door leading to his laboratory.

"Where are you going? What are you meaning to do?"

Lord Darvey waved one large, capable hand at his friend. "I'm going to write up a list, of course. Although my heart may have changed, my head hasn't. Make yourself at home, Eccleston. I shall be back soon."

In fact, nearly an hour passed before his Lordship returned to the library. He was just in time to see a footman exit the room with a tray of dirty dishes and a partially empty bottle of claret. Apparently, Mr. Eccleston had taken his friend at his word about making himself at home.

"Here it is," Lord Darvey said confidently, wafting a few stray table crumbs to the uncarpeted floor with the edge of his waving paper, "my safe-conduct to freedom."

Mr. Eccleston peered at an uncharacteristically disordered page containing a number of entries, several of which were crossed out, and arrows going in various directions. "It looks more like a code than a safe-conduct to me," he ventured. "What does it say?"

Lord Darvey smiled. "What I have here is a collection of all of the activities I could think of that Miss Brimmer and her mother would most particularly dislike. As you shall see, nothing has been too far-fetched for me to consider: keeping a private menagerie in the salon, taking in sailors' by-blows from Wapping, removing all of the furniture in the house except the beds, that sort of thing."

"I don't know why you didn't ask me to help," said Mr.

Eccleston, sounding more sulky than admiring. "I would have enjoyed working on a list like that."

"The next time I will," his Lordship said as reassuringly as though he planned to make a career of creating lists of offensive behaviors. "Don't you want to hear what I have decided upon?"

Not being a person to brood overlong, Mr. Eccleston gave an excited little bounce in his chair and said, "Fire away."

"All right, then. What does Miss Brimmer like most?"

"Her mother and brother, of course. Any nodcock can see that."

"Correct. And what does she like least?"

Mr. Eccleston hesitated but a split second before replying, "Your skulls. That's perfectly clear, too."

"Correct again. Therefore, I have put them together."

Mr. Eccleston's light brows inched up his forehead in puzzlement. "You have? That is a good idea, I'm sure, but I don't exactly see. . . ."

"It's simple." His Lordship's smile, although not precisely arrogant, was tinged with a certain pride. "I shall tell Fidelia that immediately after we marry, she and I, but not her mother or brother, will set out upon a ten-year expedition around the world in search of skulls to add to my collection. Naturally, I shall inform her, she will serve as my assistant. Well, what do you think?"

Mr. Eccleston looked at his friend with something approaching awe. "I always knew you were a smart one," he said. "Now I see that you are positively brilliant. Will you tell her today?"

Lord Darvey's lean fingers made a minute adjustment to his fine lawn neckcloth, expertly tied in a Mathematical. "Oh, no. I shan't do a thing until after I read my paper. And not even then. Since it's already too late to cancel the ball, my plan will have to be carried out during or following upon that event. I don't want any dust-ups until the whole lot is over."

"And what about Miss Hanley? Will you tell her then, as

well?" Lord Darvey nodded. "And are you certain that she will accept you?"

For the barest fraction of time, Lord Darvey looked shaken. Then he said, "She must, Eccleston, for I will not live my life without her."

"Well, then. . . ." Peter Eccleston leaped up to shake his friend's hand. "I wish you luck, Justin. Most sincerely, I do."

"Thank you." His Lordship's even white teeth flashed in a determined smile. "This time, however, I won't need luck because nothing is going to go wrong. I will not permit it to."

In truth, all seemed to be going as it ought when the momentous day of the lecture finally arrived and his Lordship and Mr. Eccleston were driven to Somerset House, that huge, impressive building on the Strand that housed the Royal Society. The richly paneled meeting room where Lord Darvey was to read his paper seemed filled nearly to capacity and included the Prince Regent and a rather surprising number of his coterie, given that they were not famous for being interested in intellectual topics. Although he was not aware of it, Lord Darvey had a reputation for daring as an explorer as well as for brilliance in his subject, which was why the meeting commanded a larger audience than it might otherwise have drawn.

He was introduced to the assemblage by Sir Joseph Banks, President of the Royal Society, attired in full court dress and wearing all of his decorations.

Lord Darvey, himself, was faultlessly attired in a black coat by Weston and form-fitting grey pantaloons. He looked competent, calm, and collected, as indeed he was—and, concerning the last two attributes, had been thus since having made up his mind what to do about Miss Brimmer and Elizabeth.

Elizabeth! But, no, now was not the time to think of her. After the ball tonight . . . that was when he would. He'd have all the time in the world then to do that and more. Soon he was going to be a very happy man.

He lowered his head to glance at the first paragraph of his paper, although every word of it had been committed to memory. As he did so, he noticed that in the second row of seats were Lord Beowulf, looking decidedly antique in a plum satin frock coat from the previous century, and some of his friends. Darvey had only a short space to wonder why they all seemed so merry. Then he forgot about them and launched into his treatise, which he'd entitled "Craniometric Differences Among the Various Races."

"It's going well," he thought, aware of the interested faces. Only the group in the second row seemed to be inattentive, particularly old Beowulf. He was squirming in his seat and had turned such an intense shade of red that Lord Darvey wondered if the man wasn't about to have an apoplectic fit.

As Lord Darvey continued his presentation, Beowulf's behavior became noticeably more peculiar. In addition to hopping up after every few points Darvey made, Lord Beowulf began to mutter, "What's that you say?" and "How is that?" in an increasingly audible voice. Only the Prince Regent's stern command to him to hold his tongue brought his mumblings to an end.

"Thus," Darvey finally got to the conclusion of his treatise, "all that can be said with any assurance at present is that there is a disparity in head size among different races but a correlation between head size and stature, that is, large people tend to have large skulls and small people to have small ones. Whether or not size has anything to do with intellect is another matter, one not within the scope of this paper."

There, he had finished. With a little bow, his Lordship put down the pages he had barely looked at and glanced composedly around the room.

"Well done." The stout Regent heaved himself with some difficulty from his chair and began applauding heartily. His words and action were repeated around the room—with the exception of Lord Beowulf's friends, who, although they had to rise because their prince had risen, stood reluctantly and remained mum.

As for Lord Beowulf, he was obviously beside himself, jerking about as though he had hot coals under his feet and waving his satin-clad arms. He was also shouting something. What it was wasn't clear in the hubbub. However, from the older man's stormy expression, it was safe to say that his words were not complimentary.

At last the applause died down and the congratulations came to an end. The return to order was followed by a call for questions. "I have one." Lord Beowulf vigorously waved his arms once more, this time, apparently, to ensure that he brought himself to Sir Joseph's immediate attention. "Your theory is nonsense. Everyone knows that we British are superior in every way to all others upon the globe."

Sir Joseph coughed and cleared his throat. "That is not a question," he said.

"Very well, then," Lord Beowulf spat, and then repeated, "Very well, then. What of your theory about small skulls and compaction, hmmm? That is a question. Tell us, what is the answer, my lord?"

Lord Darvey tilted his dark head as though that might enable him to understand the question better. "I beg your pardon?"

"You needn't pretend, my lord. I know all about your idea that people with small skulls are smarter than we Britons because their brain matter is more concentrated. Tell the truth. That is what you truly believe, isn't it? Go on. I dare you."

"The man is mad," said Mr. Eccleston in an undiplomatically loud voice.

This comment, and similar ones coming from all parts of the room, worked like oil on a blazing fire. Anger made the last traces of Lord Beowulf's discretion go up in flames. "Mad, am I?" He banged one of his pudgy fists into the other. "I'm sure you'd like to think so. However, I know Darvey believes what I said he does because I got it from his aunt's companion, who lives in his house and assists him in his work, besides. I have one of her letters here to prove it." Lord Beowulf accompanied this statement with the wave of a sheet of vellum he extracted from a deep pocket.

Mr. Eccleston's head swiveled so that he could see his friend's face, expressionless save for an ominous tautness at the lips. "What a hum," said Mr. Eccleston and gave a nervous giggle.

"Give me that." Pushing himself through the group of people around him, Darvey leaned over the first row of seats and wrested the page from Lord Beowulf. "Wait for me after the meeting," he said roughly, without looking at the paper. "We'll talk of this then."

Elizabeth thought that she would lose her wits. She had taken upon herself so much of the responsibility for the evening's events—details concerning the dinner for twenty guests preceding the ball, making sure that a footman was sent off to the florist's shop to see what had become of their order, and a hundred things more. But at least having those things to fret over was better than thinking about her departure from Grosvenor Square the following morning.

Curiously, she no longer worried about how Lord Darvey was faring in front of his audience at Somerset House. True, she had been quite overset before he walked out the door. But, then, just as he was going, he had turned to look at her, and there was such strength of character and intelligence in his grey eyes that she knew he'd be all right, yes, even if Uncle Beowulf carried on obnoxiously.

That Beowulf might do so, considering his usual behavior, she had to expect, although she did not like to contemplate it. But at least she need not fear that he would give her away—that is, she hoped she need not. To do such a thing would be sheer madness; he would be fouling his own nest.

She sighed. If it were anyone else, she would not worry about such a possibility. But since it was Uncle Beowulf, who could tell what unreasonable actions his choleric nature might urge him to?

Trying to put her concerns behind her, she let her thoughts revert once more to how his Lordship appeared when he left earlier that afternoon. She had seen something else in his eyes when he'd looked at her, a strong emotion. It had been there only an instant, and she still was not sure . . . could not really believe . . . yet it had seemed as though his eyes had been filled with love.

Becoming aware of that special warmth had been devastating.

It was a cruel enough fate to lose forever the man you loved. But how much more cruel to lose one who might return that love! Vastly unsettled by her musings, Elizabeth moved distractedly from one task to another.

She was just making a final adjustment to the flowers for the dining room table, the order having finally arrived, when Lord Darvey returned home. "Oh, you are come back," she exclaimed joyously, before she could conceal her feelings, and rushed toward him. "How did the . . . ?" She stopped abruptly and did not finish her sentence. The look of cold fury on Lord Darvey's face froze her where she stood.

In two strides, Justin Darvey was by her side. "You," he rasped at her, his darkly handsome face as hard and unyielding as a stone monolith. "You come with me." Still holding Elizabeth by the arm, he propelled her from the dining room into the library.

"What is it?" she finally found her voice and croaked. But she knew; oh, dear God, she knew. There could only be one explanation for the way his Lordship was treating her—her uncle had decided to throw caution to the winds and tell Lord Darvey what she—and he—had done.

Along with the grief and regret, fear spread through her, emanating in waves into her limbs from the cold lump in her belly. The Lord Darvey she had fallen in love with, as tolerant and pleasant as he was rational, was not one whit in evidence. He had been replaced by that wild Lord Darvey who had raged at her because she'd gone off to meet her brother without telling him, and then had rushed out to do battle with Mr. Brimmer's friends. Only it was more dreadful than that, because this time all of the passion and temper she'd been made aware of then in his nature were ensheathed in ice; it burned worse than any fire could.

"It's true, isn't it?" his Lordship said, the question really a statement. "You're Beowulf's niece, and you came here to spy on me for him.

"What?" he demanded sharply when she made a sound he could barely hear. "What did you say?"

Elizabeth bent her head so that the vulnerable skin at the back of her neck showed around her auburn curls. She mumbled, "I said yes; it's true."

"Is that all? Look at me," his Lordship commanded, lifting her chin with punishing fingers. "Why did you do it?"

Elizabeth tried to turn her head so that she would not have to see the familiar face, now devoid not only of love but also of gentleness. He would not let her, though.

"Answer me," he said grimly. "I'm waiting."

Answer him? Yes, she would have to, and now, all of a sudden, she was glad of it. She would confess everything, and even if he struck her, which he looked as though he might wish to do, she would at least have regained her integrity in some small measure. That would be something. She would take that with her, and that would be what she would have.

"Cold comfort." The words she had once thought in her futile effort to convince herself not to be attracted to him formed again in her mind. She tossed her head as though that way she could dislodge them.

When she looked at him, her luminous green eyes were wide and shimmering with tears that she was too proud to let fall. "I did it to help my brother and myself," she said, forcing herself to look directly into his cutting grey gaze, "although I do not offer that as an excuse; it is just a fact. Uncle Beowulf agreed to give David a letter of recommendation, you see, so that David could get work somewhere else, if I promised to spy on you. But I should not have been willing to do it even for the opportunity to get away from Uncle."

"Do not think that you can get around me with pathetic stories and hysterical weeping." Lord Darvey's voice was harsh, but the gesture of his hand plucking at one of the ebony buttons that marched down his coat suggested that he was perhaps not altogether easy in his attitude. "What you did was despicable, and if you were a man I would thrash you or worse. Tell me, did your brother know of this plot? Of course, he must have. I shall find him and kill him."

"Oh, no, you must not." The tears finally spilled over and ran down Elizabeth's pale, silky skin. "It wasn't his fault. He begged me, he ordered me, not to go, but I would not listen so determined was I to achieve our release from Uncle Beowulf's domination." She did not mention that once David had become enamored of Lady Thea, he had begged Elizabeth just as strongly to remain at her post. He had done that because he had fallen in love. It was a reason for which she felt complete sympathy.

Lord Darvey removed a large white handkerchief from the pocket in his coat. "Here." He extended it to her without touching her. "Wipe your face, and stop that. You won't change my feelings about you and your mongrel tribe that way, you know." He hesitated and then said, "I can never forgive you for your falsity, Miss Hanley—if that is your real name."

Elizabeth's hands twisted into the handkerchief; then she forced them to be still against her sides. "It is. That is one thing I told you that is true at least. And that I never really meant to do harm to you, that also is a true thing, although I know that you do not care. I . . . I even vowed to

Primrose before we left Epsom that I would somehow make amends to you one day."

"Did you, indeed? And how did you mean to do that?"

Elizabeth bit at her full lower lip before she answered, "I do not know."

"Nor do I," Lord Darvey said arctically, "because you can't. Nor will you have the opportunity even if you could. I never wish to see you again, Miss Hanley, and as soon as this ball is over, I want you out of the house and out of my life."

"I will go now."

Elizabeth could have sworn that Lord Darvey's breath caught at her words. All he said, though, was a sharp, "Indeed, you won't. You will remain and attend my aunt at the ball tonight. Then you will go, and good riddance."

She had meant to leave the next morning, anyway. Nothing had changed, she told herself with a bravado that barely lasted the time it took her to form the thought. "If you wish it." Shoulders sloping as though they carried the world's sorrows upon them as well as her own, Elizabeth turned and began to walk toward the door.

"Wait!"

"Yes, my lord?"

"Why did you tell your uncle that bizarre story that I believed people with small heads are superior beings? That is the most preposterous thing I have ever heard."

Was that the hint of a smile on Lord Darvey's tightly held lips? No, she must have imagined it. "It is preposterous, isn't it?" she agreed with a rueful smile. "I invented it to put him off after he took your paper. I wanted to ensure that he would not believe he had your true theory, so I said that you had changed your ideas. Then I made up that nonsense, and he believed it."

"So he did steal my paper. Of course, I knew it. Why did you not want him to have the truth?"

"How could I?" Elizabeth's voice unconsciously softened. "It might have done harm to you. I know that you do not believe me, but I swear, my lord, I never wanted Uncle Beowulf's plot to succeed . . . especially after I got to know you."

"And why is that?" Lord Darvey put out a firm, tanned hand to touch Elizabeth, but then he let it drop. "Never mind." His look was steely. "I do not want to know. Remember, you must stay until after the ball. Then you must leave."

"If it pleases you." Elizabeth made a little curtsy and walked from the room.

Left alone in the library, Lord Darvey bent his head and groaned into his hands. "It doesn't please me, absurd fool that I am. God help me, but it doesn't please me at all."

He sat alone like that for some time, not lifting his head except to order an occasional footman who wandered in to leave the room. The thick walls insulated him from the preparations for the ball going forward in the rooms nearby. Only the sounds made by the tall satinwood grandfather clock talking to itself punctured his thoughts. From the look on his face, those thoughts remained unhappy ones.

What an irony it was that his taste of triumph had turned to ashes in his mouth. He would have felt better if he had kept his illusions, and his love, even at the cost of a commendation for his work from the entire Royal Society. In the past—by which he meant before he had fallen in love with Elizabeth—he would never have believed that he would some day be willing to turn down the approval of his peers for the love of a woman. For the love of one woman.

When at last he straightened in his chair, his expression, if not serene, was one of resolution. "Even though I am not to have Elizabeth, I still will not have Fidelia," he told himself. "Tonight, I will tell her that I mean to make her travel the globe with me. She will break it off, and then I will go away—alone—and travel the world by myself. By the time I return, I will have forgotten all about Elizabeth Hanley. Why, I will not even remember her name."

He was lying; he knew it. With all his talk of truth this

day, now he was lying, too. He could never forgive
Elizabeth for her deceitfulness, but he would never forget
the smallest thing about her, either. Her low, faintly husky
voice; her smooth skin and unconsciously provocative red
lips; even her perfume that smelled like newly budded
roses—all sounds, sights, and aromas he associated with
her were etched into his soul. Still, if a lie could help him
to get through the next hours without giving away his
anguished feelings, he embraced it. This night he would
need every resource he could command.

Eleven

ALTHOUGH MISS BRIMMER looked charming, indeed, dressed in a silk gown of celestial blue with aerophane net oversleeves and a surprisingly brief bodice, she was not smiling. And that was noteworthy because smiling was something she could nearly always be counted upon to do.

"I fear I do not understand you, my lord," she addressed Lord Darvey, her pretty, vague face looking more unfocused than usual. "Are you saying that you wish me to spend some time with you on a boat?"

"Ship," corrected Lord Darvey, looking most attractive himself in an exquisitely tailored black coat, pantaloons, and striped silk stockings that showed his well-developed calves to advantage.

"Would that be our bridetrip?" Miss Brimmer asked doubtfully.

His Lordship made a slight adjustment to his white marcella waistcoat before saying, "No, that would be our life. We'll sail from port to port and live on the ship, only going ashore to collect specimens or when we need to replenish our supplies. Doesn't it sound grand?"

"Ummm." Miss Brimmer blinked her pale blue eyes. "I do not believe Mama and Barton would care for it."

"Then we will not take them along." Lord Darvey accompanied his words with an agreeable smile.

Miss Brimmer's soft lower lip trembled. "But that would mean that we would not see them for quite a long time."

"That is exactly right. Not for ten years, at least."

"Ten years! Oh, no, I couldn't!"

Giving Miss Brimmer a bracing pat on the back, his Lordship said, "But of course you could. Trust me, my dear.

"And do not worry about the cannibals and headhunters," he added in a scarcely audible voice.

"What?"

"Oh, nothing."

Miss Brimmer favored him with another doubtful glance.

"You mustn't overlook the skulls, either," Lord Darvey said, as though they would make all the difference, which, indeed, he hoped that they would. "What with collecting and cataloguing them, you will have so much to keep you occupied that you'll have quite a good time and never miss your family at all."

Although the grand salon, with its crush of people, was more than adequately warm, Miss Brimmer shivered. "No," she said as firmly as she had ever said anything in her life, "I couldn't do those things."

"Are you certain?"

Her nod was unequivocal.

"Well, then. . . ." Lord Darvey sighed with a melancholy that he did, indeed, feel even if it had nothing to do with this woman. "What's to be done? I will not change my mind."

"Oh, look there." Miss Brimmer pointed a daintily gloved finger toward a group of young men. "It is Lord North. He has been visiting us quite a bit lately, nearly every day. He is very nice."

"How—nice." Lord Darvey's voice had an ironic tinge that Miss Brimmer almost certainly missed. "Why don't you go and speak to him? I am certain that he would like that since he must be fond of you."

"Do you think so?" For the first time, Miss Brimmer

smiled. "I rather thought that myself, although Mama said. . . . Never mind. I believe I will just walk in his direction. He loathes skulls, you know."

This parting remark gave Lord Darvey some hope that his plan might work after all, considering his fiancée's decided aversion to his occupation. Add to that Lord North's very pressing needs—his Lordship smiled wryly to himself. As Eccleston had said at the first, Darvey's best hope was to find someone to take his place with Miss Brimmer. Lord North might well be that person.

And if not, and if Miss Brimmer still wished to keep up the engagement, then he, Darvey, would break it off, let all the world call him a cad. Yes, although he still had reason to worry, Lord Darvey had some hope.

But no joy. Joy was Elizabeth, and she was not for him.

As the orchestra struck up a waltz, he saw Lord North bow to Miss Brimmer and she smilingly accept him as her partner. Lord Darvey watched them move about the floor for awhile.

Then he turned his dark head toward the row of gilt chairs against the south wall, where he knew, from several surreptitious glances, that Elizabeth sat with his great aunt, who was so wrapped up it looked as if Elizabeth guarded a mummy.

She, herself, was beautiful in a glossy green lutestring gown that accentuated her pale, lustrous skin and green eyes. Without success, he tried to hold down the love and longing that swamped him in defiance of his inclinations.

As though she felt the pull of his emotions across the room, he saw her look up and discover his gaze upon her. He sensed, rather than observed, her flush. Then she tucked in the fine wool shawl she was adding to the layers about Lady Treadway's shoulders and walked rapidly from the room.

Brushing aside those guests who tried to engage him in conversation, Lord Darvey followed her. He was prepared to track her to her rooms or wherever else she might have run, although he hadn't the faintest inkling what he would say to her.

He came upon her just outside the library, where she had been halted with a question by one of the footmen. She was standing half-turned away from Darvey so that he glimpsed part of her smooth, lovely back, and she was shifting her yellow-slippered feet in uneasy impatience.

When she saw Darvey, she put her slender fingers to her mouth, dropping her reticule in the process. "I am on an errand," she said nervously, oblivious of the fallen bag.

Lord Darvey's calm voice was roughened by feelings he could not altogether submerge. "No wait. You must not go yet."

"Why . . . why not?"

"Because I mean to have you dance with me, Elizabeth— this one time if never again." Heedless of the people who stood nearby, he took her into his arms.

"My lord, what are you about?" she asked, attempting to move away from him.

Ignoring her efforts, his Lordship said, "The first time I saw you, when you came to apply for the position with my great aunt, you fell over Primrose's cage. Do you remember that?" Elizabeth blushed and nodded.

"I told Eccleston then that it did not matter if you were a trifle clumsy, for I never meant to dance with you. But I lied, Elizabeth. I've wanted to hold you like this from the very moment I saw you." His grey eyes darkened to the color of coal. "Make up your mind to it, for I will not be refused."

His strong, clever hands tightened at her waist and shoulder, and he pulled her closer so that through her dress the tops of her breasts brushed against his black coat. Then he waltzed her into the library.

One, two, three; one, two, three; the sweet, lilting music followed them. Justin and Elizabeth moved as a single being in measured circuits across the polished parquet floor. Her rose perfume mingled with the heady male odors of brandy and musk that clung to him. Neither of them spoke.

Then the pace of the music quickened. The sentimental sounds of the first part changed and became rich with passionate feeling. Their bodies responded to the difference, and they whirled about the floor in looser, wider circles. Justin's hand at Elizabeth's waist spread until the tips of his fingers lay under her breast.

Gazing down at her pink-tinged face, he commanded, "Look at me," but she lowered her silky brown lashes over her eyes instead. "Look at me," he repeated insistently.

Reluctantly, Elizabeth tilted her chin and stared directly up at his Lordship. He did not seem quite so cold and angry as when he'd returned from the meeting, she thought. In fact, there was a gleam in his eyes that almost made her think he had some softer feeling for her.

Lord Darvey's jaw tensed, and then, without warning, he bent his head and kissed Elizabeth so hard on the mouth that her lips were pressed back against her teeth.

Ah, now she knew what that gleam meant. He despised her and meant to take his revenge on her by treating her like Haymarket ware.

With a tortured expression, she looked into his storm-swirled grey eyes. "I have not forgotten that you hate me, my lord," she said in a near whisper, "and can never forgive me. I want you to know that I understand and do not blame you. I also want you to know that I am sorrier than I can say."

"How can I forgive you?" Lord Darvey's expression was as tortured as her own, but he tightened his grasp on her as he spoke. "What you did was unpardonable."

Elizabeth unconsciously licked her ripe, bruised lips. "Oh, it was."

"Even if I forgave you, I could never trust you again. You've shattered my faith in you."

The pink tip of Elizabeth's tongue touched the outer corners of her mouth in agitation. "You are absolutely right."

"Oh, hell." As though of its own volition, his mouth covered hers once more.

There, she thought desperately, he was doing it again. Perhaps he meant even to seduce her. But as much as she deserved punishment, and as much as she might hunger to be seduced, God help her, she could not let him do it.

Pushing him away, she said grimly, "My lord, you must not."

"No." Lord Darvey took a few steps backward as though recoiling from the edge of a precipice that both repelled and invited. "You are right," he said. "I mustn't."

Once again, he began to dance with her. Faster and faster—faster, even, than the music that faintly drifted in to them—they spun across the smooth floor. The red and blue books that lined the walls blended for them into a single band of pulsating color.

When they had made a complete turn about the room, Lord Darvey brought them to an abrupt halt. "Damn it, Elizabeth," he groaned; "damn you. It doesn't matter what you've done or who your rabid relatives are. I cannot help myself." He wrapped both arms around her and kissed her dimple-edged mouth until it was completely atingle with stirring sensations.

"Dear me. Do, pray, excuse us." Smiling vacuously, Miss Brimmer stood in the open doorway to the library along with Lord North. "Would you prefer that we come back later, when you are less engaged? *Engaged!*" she repeated and giggled.

Lord Darvey put Elizabeth away from him and beckoned his fiancée to come in. "Leave us, North," he ordered. "Fidelia, we need to talk."

"I shan't leave," Lord North said tensely, closing the door behind them. "I have a right to be here with Miss Brimmer."

Intent upon his speech, he failed to see the interested look his words brought to Lord Darvey's face. North cleared his throat noisily, then continued, "Let me say first that we don't care what you do with the help. Although why Miss Hanley would reject my suit for—but never mind that, either. We have come to tell you something, and from the position you are in, Darvey, I cannot see that you have any right to object."

"Oh?" Lord Darvey tugged nonchalantly at one of the cuffs of his shirt until it was neatly exposed below his coat sleeve. "And since when have you involved yourself with my fiancée's affairs?"

Elizabeth gave his Lordship a reproachful look. He should be apologizing profusely instead of baiting Lord North. Well, if he wouldn't apologize, she would. Hadn't she caused enough trouble?

"I am deeply sorry, Miss Brimmer. It was my fault," she said, happy to sacrifice even her good name in order to help the man she dearly loved, not to mention had most dreadfully wronged.

"Oh, I don't mind." Miss Brimmer nullified the sacrifice.

"Truly?" Elizabeth looked stunned. How generous Miss Brimmer was. If it had been she, she'd have. . . . Wild-eyed, Elizabeth gazed at the others, then sobbed once very loudly and ran from the room.

"The devil!" Lord Darvey started to go after her but was stopped by a determined Lord North blocking his path.

"You can chase her later," Lord North said. "For now, please listen. I don't have much time, you know."

"It's true, Darvey." Although she addressed him, Miss Brimmer appeared to be staring over his shoulder. "The fact is, I cannot possibly marry you, not just because of my mother and brother, but because of the boat and the skulls and the things you did not want me to hear. No matter how I try, I cannot make myself like them."

Shifting her glance so that she was staring over Lord North's shoulder, she said, "He doesn't like them, either, and won't have them. Also, he needs a wife, and since it is clear that you and I do not suit, I am agreeable to it, even though Mama doesn't precisely care for him. So, if you don't mind too much. . . ."

"Nor does it matter if you do," Lord North added boldly. "Miss Brimmer is now engaged to me, and we'll be married tomorrow, since I just happen to have a special license in my rooms."

"Far be it from me to hinder the course of true love," Lord Darvey said sardonically and escorted them back to the salon.

Once there, he looked about benevolently. He was very pleased with himself. He had explained his feelings and good intentions to Elizabeth, and he'd got rid of his peagoose of a fiancée.

A sliver of worry penetrated the fat cloud of his complacency. He had made himself clear to Elizabeth before the others had barged in, hadn't he? Of course, she must have understood that he loved her and meant to marry her.

He looked down uncomfortably at his hands. Then why would she have sobbed and run off so precipitously? He knew that females sometimes behaved incomprehensibly when they were very happy, but, somehow, he doubted that this was one of those times. Perhaps Elizabeth did not know that he loved her after all. Further, she wasn't aware that he was no longer engaged. Well, as soon as these people cleared out. . . . He looked with disfavor upon his friends and fellow members of the Royal Society still milling about in the salon, and was not even able to call up a smile for Lady Thea, who did not look particularly happy herself.

Seeing her, it came to him that David Hanley was not there. Somehow, either through Lord Beowulf or Elizabeth, David must have learned that he was *persona non grata* in Grosvenor Square. Of course, Justin would have to forgive David eventually since the latter would be his brother.

If only these people would leave, Lord Darvey thought once more. But, most of them chose not to depart until it was quite late. What was more, with one thing and another, such as dancing with the females on whose cards he had been fool enough to scratch his name earlier, he was kept too occupied to step out even for a little while to seek Elizabeth. He was hard put to behave civilly to his guests.

By the time the last guests finally said their farewells, he decided he had better wait until the morning to talk to Elizabeth; he did not have the heart to wake her. Now, if only he could sleep.

Eventually, he did, but his sleep was unsatisfying, laced as it was with various stimulating if ultimately frustrating dreams in which he glimpsed parts of her beauty which then disappeared. When he finally awoke, it was near to eight o'clock, and he had a deuce of a headache.

Still, it was nothing compared to the one he developed when he discovered that, although the clothes that had been purchased for her were still in her bedroom, Elizabeth and Primrose had gone from the house.

David had sent a note to Elizabeth the night of the ball that he would collect her at eight o'clock the next morning and return her to Epsom. Despite having no reason to believe that Uncle Beowulf would welcome her back, she meant to go to his house anyway, to obtain David's letter of recommendation and a few trinkets that had belonged to her mother. After that, she thought morosely, she did not care where she went. Without Justin Darvey, she had no real home.

She meant to leave at once but instead found herself walking to the laboratory. She'd go "just one more time," she thought, to say a final farewell to the place where she had been so happy.

She wondered if the years would fade her memories of it. She had nothing to keep as a memento. Elizabeth let her eyes wander about the room, looking for something whose absence would not matter. There was only the lead shot. Beggars can't afford to be choosers, she thought. Hastily, she filled up her pockets.

The sky was overcast, and it was still chilly out-of-doors, making her glad that she had donned her thick, old brown cloak, faded and ugly as it was. Besides, it had capacious pockets. She inserted one hand to feel the shot.

Naturally, she had not taken the cloak or any of the other things his Lordship had bought her, although it had not been easy to leave them behind. She thought of them as ill-gotten gains to which she had no right.

She had no right to Lord Darvey, either. The thought made her throat close. Standing there at the curb with Primrose, she started to cry. She cried so hard that she could not see. If it had not been for the clop-clopping of the horses' hooves on the cobbles, she wouldn't have been aware of the approaching carriage.

"The coachman will need to stow my portmanteau," she blubbered, after handing up Primrose's cage and then blindly feeling her way into the interior of the closed carriage. "Let us be off; I can't bear to tarry another minute."

"Neither can I."

The man's voice, although familiar, was certainly not that of her brother. Hastily wiping her eyes on an edge of her cloak, Elizabeth looked up—and into the plump, dissipated face of Barton Brimmer. It was creased in a smile, but it was not a reassuring smile.

"What luck," he said, before taking a swig from a nearly empty wine bottle. "I couldn't have planned it better."

"Let me get down," said Elizabeth—but he gave her a blow to the head instead, rendering her unconscious.

Mr. Brimmer looked cheerfully at his unheeding victim. "Naturally, I don't like to hit women, but I owed you that one," he said. Then he added, "We won't need this," and threw the bird cage out of the window.

"Gor," said a passing chimney sweep with a permanently dirty face as he dropped his brooms to catch it. "Gor."

A worried-looking Mr. Herbert, the same Mr. Herbert who had been Lord Darvey's opponent at fisticuffs in the latter's garden, climbed clumsily down from the box where he'd been sitting beside his liveried coachman and peered into the carriage. "What's up?" he asked. "I thought we were going to go to bed."

"We are," Mr. Brimmer smiled and said in a suggestive, oily tone, "with the addition of some charming company. Get rid of your coachman, Herbert, and spring it."

"What? Where to?"

Impatiently, Mr. Brimmer waved a pale, freckled hand. "To my house in Wimbledon. Hurry, man. We can't stand here and discuss it."

Away they went, and the coachman, recognizing something havey cavey when he saw it, quickly vanished as well. Only the little sweep, unable to decide whether to run off with Primrose or see what he could filch from the portmanteau, lingered.

Before the boy could make up his mind what to do with his booty, David pulled up to the curb. Erupting from his house, Lord Darvey was scant seconds behind.

"Where is Elizabeth?" they asked each other in chorus, then, still as one, directed their eyes to the sweep. While David jumped down from his rented coach, his Lordship advanced on the boy. "What are you doing with that bird?" he asked menacingly, "and where is the lady who owns it?"

"I didn't do nothing," the boy blurted, his soot-stained fingers letting go of poor Primrose's cage. As quick as lightning, Lord Darvey grabbed it before it could touch the ground. "It was them blokes took her, a big one fat as a flawn and a little grinnin' one with yeller hair and his eyes all red."

The sweep cast about for something more to tell them to continue to distract the tall man with the murderous expression from his own small person. "The big one's name was 'Erbert," he said happily, having found another scrap to throw to the lion, "and they was going to the other's house, in Wimbledon, I think was wot he said. That's all I remember, m'lords, truly."

Lord Darvey threw down some coins for him, then turned to David. "Take this," he said, handing the younger man Primrose's cage and ignoring the portmanteau, "and put it in the house. Then get the grooms to give you my curricle. I'm going by horseback; it will be faster. To Wimbledon, Hanley!"

Naturally, Elizabeth was unaware that her would-be rescuers were on their way. All she knew was that she was deeply in trouble, alone in a house with an unprincipled man, and had no one but herself to rely upon. She would need to think of something to do, a difficult task in her situation at the best of times but near-impossible given the dreadful headache which accompanied her return to consciousness.

"Ah, awake, are you?" A leering Barton Brimmer peered down at her. "Welcome to my little love nest."

Although Elizabeth had never before been to any place the least bit unrespectable, she could well imagine orgies being conducted here. It was all the red—walls, floor, and furniture—the gaudy mirrors, and especially the marble statues of naked men and women doing embarrassing things to each other. She shuddered.

"Are you cold?" Mr. Brimmer asked with patently false solicitousness. "Don't know how you could be in that heavy cloak. It must weigh a ton, or you're a lot fatter than you look. Well, we'll warm you up soon enough."

As if that statement weren't distressing enough to her, Elizabeth saw with dismay that another man, a very big man, had come into the room. "So, who did I carry in here, Brimmer?" He peered at her more closely, then asked, "Never say that's the young lady who lives in Darvey's house?"

He listened to Mr. Brimmer's reply, then spat, "I told you not to say it! You must be crazy to get us mixed up with him. Didn't you hear what he did to me at our mill in his garden?"

Mr. Brimmer's laugh held only a little fear. "I'm not afraid of him, and nor should you be. He doesn't know we have her, and he doesn't know where we are."

"Is that so?" Mr. Herbert's beefy face relaxed. Then it tightened again. "But what do you mean to do with her afterward? I won't be a party to any violence on a female."

"You've got to stop fretting yourself. We're going to make Miss Hanley have such a grand time that she won't have anything to complain about to anyone. In fact, she won't want to leave us."

This remark seemed to cheer Mr. Herbert immensely. With an awkward gait, like that of a sailor not yet in possession of his sea legs, he started to walk toward Elizabeth.

She had to do something now, though that was easier to say than to accomplish. Gingerly, for the sake of her head, she got up from the couch. As she did so, her hand struck one of the pockets in her cloak. It was heavy with lead shot. She filled her hands with it, then threw it upon the floor in the path of the advancing Mr. Herbert.

"What's this?" he cried, slipping and sliding on a wave of lead balls. A second later, his feet went out from under him and he was down. Like the wreck of some colossus, he lay there, groaning piteously.

Mr. Brimmer thrust Elizabeth back upon the couch, then, making his way carefully, went to kneel beside his friend. "What is it, Herbert? What has she done to you?"

"It's my leg." Mr. Herbert's high color faded until he looked pale and sick. "I think it's broken."

"Broken? It can't be. How are we going to have fun with this jade if you've gone and broken your leg? Get up, man. Stop being the skeleton at the feast."

"I'll be a skeleton soon enough if you don't get me a doctor," Mr. Herbert whined. "A broken leg is serious."

Mr. Brimmer scowled. "I can't bring a doctor here, Herbert. You're not thinking. How am I going to explain

Miss Hanley, especially if she decides to complain that I've given her Turkish treatment?"

"Don't blame the Turks!" Elizabeth snapped, speaking up even though she had promised herself to remain mute and try to avoid bringing notice to herself. "This whole bumblebroth is your fault. What is more, you had better take this man to a doctor at once, else he might become permanently crippled or lose his leg."

"Take him? I can't do that, either," Mr. Brimmer responded over his friend's cries of alarm. "I could never lift him. Blast it, I suppose I'll have to fetch a doctor here after all. Now, what shall I do with you?"

Elizabeth gave him what she hoped appeared a cooperative smile. "Why, nothing. I'll spend my time while you're gone picking up the shot. And I'll minister to poor Mr. Herbert by bringing him drinks and cold cloths and the like. When I hear your carriage returning, I'll go into another room."

Mr. Brimmer cocked a pale eyebrow at her. "You must take me for a flat. I could not trust you to remain here a minute after I'd gone. No, I'll sweep up the shot, and it's trussing and gagging for you, my girl. Now all I need to do is find some rope and some cloth. Herbert," he demanded, "do we have anything like that in the carriage?"

If he expected an answer, he did not get one. The numbness Mr. Herbert experienced when first he injured his leg was passing off and was being replaced by severe pain. He had no interest in esoteric things such as ropes and gags.

"Very well." Mr. Brimmer rose from his friend's side and began to pick nervously at his vest, embroidered in pink cabbage roses. "I shall lock you in my bedroom, Miss Hanley. And if you start to scream or that sort of thing when the doctor comes, I shall tell him that you are mad, and then I shall beat you. Just think about that."

Elizabeth did think about it, and about Lord Darvey and the whereabouts of her pet, since the bedroom did not offer her a means of egress. The windows were too high to jump from, and she could not force the locked door open, although she bruised herself running against it in her efforts to knock it down.

What to do? Mr. Brimmer was a curious mix of bully and buffoon, so she could not determine how he might behave next or what tactics might work best against him. That he meant to have her, though, she did not doubt.

Since she could not escape, she would have to defend herself; there had to be something she could use as a weapon. She looked carefully around the room. It seemed as much a mix as Mr. Brimmer. The wide bed and the other furnishings were luxurious, even sybaritic, with their fine inlaid woods and bright purple silks and velvets. But then there were the other items, incongruous things such as a set of toy soldiers, a drum, and a collection of swords and daggers.

Daggers! That was it. She would have to stab him. She knew that if she could first pick out the right spot on Mr. Brimmer and then close her eyes, she could manage it.

Perhaps she had better keep her eyes open. She could always be sick later, she thought. The important thing to remember was to do the deed as soon as he came into the room. She might not have a second chance.

When she heard the doctor's carriage pull up, she prepared herself by making several passes with the most vicious-looking weapon in the collection, a jewel-handled dagger with a sharp, glinting blade. If she meant to do it, there must be no nonsense about it. She went to stand beside the door and wait.

She stood thus for several minutes and then, when nothing happened, relaxed her guard. She should have realized that Mr. Brimmer would not come up until the doctor left. Well, she was prepared now. Just let him dare to attempt to molest her.

In fact, Elizabeth was mistaken in believing that Mr. Brimmer had gone upon his errand, although he soon wished he had. When Lord Darvey burst into the house, looking like an avenging angel, with David Hanley not far behind, Mr. Brimmer accepted the distinct possibility that he was going to need the services of a doctor, if not a grave digger, for himself.

"What are you doing here," he asked in a quavering voice, "and how did you find me?"

"We asked; you're infamous. What have you done with Elizabeth?" Darvey spared only one glance for the fallen Mr. Herbert, then ignored him.

"I haven't done anything," Mr. Brimmer said sullenly. "She went and broke old Herbert's leg, so I've had to attend to him and haven't had a chance to. . . ." His voice trailed off. Even he was able to realize that it wasn't politic to voice his intentions to his Lordship and her brother. "She's upstairs, locked in my room."

His Lordship's grim expression lightened a trifle. "Did she really do that?" he asked proudly, pointing to Herbert. "Good girl."

"Right," Mr. Brimmer said ingratiatingly. "She's still a good girl. No harm's been done. So why don't you collect her and forget this whole thing? We're going to be brothers soon, after all."

"Indeed we are not," said Lord Darvey, "or haven't you heard? Not that it would matter anyway, Brimmer."

"No, it wouldn't," David interrupted, his face almost as darkly red as his hair. He took a step toward the miscreant. "I'll tear off your head, you overstuffed partridge."

"No need, Hanley." Lord Darvey stepped with Olympian dignity between them. "I'll handle this. Besides, I think you should go for the doctor. Old Herbert isn't looking very well. We wouldn't want Elizabeth to be blamed for any possible complications he might suffer."

David frowned. "I suppose that's true, but shouldn't I at least free her first?"

"Don't give it a thought," Lord Darvey, still looking dignified, said reassuringly. "It will take me a minute to clear up our little problem here. Then I shall find her. Go along and do not concern yourself."

When he heard the door close behind David, his Lordship's calm demeanor disappeared as though it had never been. "Now, Brimmer," he said with a ferocious growl, "I'm going to make you sorry that you were ever born. But, first, tell me, are you wearing a corset?"

"Certainly not." In spite of his evident fear, Mr. Brimmer looked offended. Then he added, "Are you sure that you don't want to talk about this?"

Lord Darvey's smile was not a pretty thing to see. "No. I mean first to maul you in several places, and then I mean to do away with you; talking isn't in my plans at all."

Mr. Brimmer whirled around and grabbed a long piece of wood standing upright in the fireplace basket. He held it between his hands as though to show Lord Darvey what the latter was up against. "Just try it," he said, apparently deciding that he had nothing to lose.

Twelve

LORD DARVEY MADE several distinctly unBritish sounds, and his fists flashed. The next thing Mr. Brimmer knew, the piece of wood was two pieces of wood, both lying on the floor, and his hands stung like the devil.

His plump visage lost its color and became a disbelieving white mask. "Good God," he cried, "what are you doing? You never learned that at Gentleman Jackson's."

"Indeed not." Lord Darvey's darkly handsome face wore a well-pleased, if disquieting, smile. "It's a way of fighting I learned in the Orient. I had wondered if there would ever be a situation in this country in which I'd feel free to use it. Now there is." He paused, then added, "Perhaps I should thank you for giving me this opportunity—but I don't think I will."

Instead of commenting on his Lordship's explanation, Mr. Brimmer said quickly, "Look there!" and gestured toward Mr. Herbert. Warily, Darvey skewed his eyes toward his former opponent, still lying in a stout heap on the floor. Seizing his opportunity, Mr. Brimmer swung his fist.

His Lordship easily parried the punch. Then he struck Mr. Brimmer several times across the head, causing the shorter man to lurch like a top. While Mr. Brimmer was thus spirally occupied, Lord Darvey braced one leg behind the other, turned the palms of his hands outward, and curled his fingertips.

"What are you doing now?" Mr. Brimmer said shrilly.

His Lordship spoke through his gleaming, white teeth. "Tiger position. I'm going to tear you apart, just like a tiger."

"Don't you dare," screamed Mr. Brimmer. "You'll kill me."

"Yes, that's what I said I'd do. Have you forgotten so soon? But I need to maul you a little first."

His Lordship moved his elegant, lethal hands back and forth several times while Mr. Brimmer watched in dumbfounded fascination. Then the hands did several quick, unpleasant things to Mr. Brimmer's torso, followed by a kick which knocked the blond man's legs out from under him.

The would-be ravisher came to rest on an obscenely red rug near where Mr. Herbert reposed. After that, only an occasional spasmodic movement, like that of a played-out fish, gave evidence that Mr. Brimmer was still among the living. "That will teach you to trifle with my Elizabeth," said Lord Darvey. Not bothering to shut the door behind him, he sped from the room.

Elizabeth heard the heavy thud of his boots racing up the marble stairs. Not knowing that his Lordship was in the house, however, she assumed that the boots were on Mr. Brimmer and wondered why her kidnapper was displaying intemperate haste in getting to her. Such impatience assuredly boded ill, she told herself with a shudder.

Now the fool was tearing down the hall, banging open doors. Couldn't he remember where he had put her? No matter. She shifted the wicked-looking dagger to her right hand and took a deep breath. She was ready for anything.

Still, when the bedroom door went flying off its hinges and landed nearly across the room, she had all she could do not to drop her weapon. "Take that, you rogue," she cried, and mercilessly gave the intruder a good cut just below his shoulder.

"Blister it, Elizabeth," Lord Darvey sounded as cross as crabs, "why did you do that?"

Elizabeth's dagger fell from her nerveless fingers to lie in barbarically jeweled splendor upon the floor. Slowly, she sank down to join it and leaned back against the wall. She felt light-headed and wondered if she was going to faint. Although she had never fainted before, she rather hoped she would this time. It would be better to sprawl unconscious on the rug than have to face a man you had lied to, spied on, lusted after, and now stabbed, a man, moreover, who hated you and never wanted to see you again.

His Lordship knelt beside her. "Are you all right?"

"Am *I* all right?" she asked with embarrassment. "Of course I am, but are you?"

When his Lordship nodded and sat carefully beside her, she said, "I thought you were someone else."

"I should hope so." Although he still appeared to be irritated, Lord Darvey's grey eyes glittered with amusement.

Elizabeth twisted her hands into the skirts of the old green round gown she had donned that morning. "Are you sure I did not hurt you?"

Before answering, his Lordship took out a handkerchief and wadded it, then slipped it inside his shirt. "It's nothing," he said, looking at her unhappy face. "And I thought I told you a long time ago to dispose of that ugly dress."

Elizabeth seemed not to have heard his criticism of her attire. "Oh, what have I done?"

"Defended yourself well, I'd say." His Lordship grinned, making the final traces of his ill-humor vanish. "You are a courageous woman, Elizabeth, as well as a beautiful one. I am proud of you."

He was so close. She could feel his soft, curly hair against her face and smell his starched linen. His warm, clean breath caressed her neck. She was in heaven! She was in hell!

"W— . . . What did you do to Mr. Brimmer?" she asked, barely aware of the sense of the words she stumbled over.

Lord Darvey leaned on her a little. "If you were looking at him now, you wouldn't need to ask. He's on the floor, next to Herbert."

"Are you certain that you're all right?" Elizabeth asked anxiously.

His Lordship said a bit impatiently, "I'll be fine until the doctor arrives. Now, why don't you tell me what you did to Mr. Herbert? I assume you did not break his leg with your dainty hands—or did you?" He accompanied his words by very gently lifting her left hand and running a hard thumb across the back of it.

It was so nice being stroked like that, Elizabeth thought. If she had been a cat, she would have purred. She would have been content to stay thus forever. In fact, she forgot that Lord Darvey was waiting for her explanation until he stopped rubbing her hand and tapped it lightly to get her attention.

When she explained what she had done, he started to laugh. Smiling, Elizabeth said, "Of course, it's lucky that I had the shot in my pockets; otherwise, I'm not certain what I might have managed."

"You'd have thought of something," his Lordship said lazily, "but why did you?"

Why did she have the shot? That was a reasonable question. It was too bad that she did not have a reasonable answer. Sometimes it seemed to Elizabeth that her whole time in Lord Darvey's house had been spent in making up or avoiding answers to perilous questions. "Why did I what, my lord?"

"Why were your pockets full of shot?"

Elizabeth gave him a disingenuous smile. "I've been wondering that very thing myself. The only conclusion I can come to that makes the least bit of sense is that Primrose put it there; it's just the sort of thing he would do."

Before his Lordship could question this dubious proposition, she asked, hesitating as though afraid to hear the answer, "He is all right, isn't he? I've worried so about him, in between all of my other worries."

Moved by the thought of what she must have suffered, Lord Darvey started to put his arm around her. He gave up on the effort when he saw her stiffen.

"Is it bad news?" she asked quietly, the words forcing their way between her tight, grim lips.

"Oh, is that what you thought? Nothing of the sort. Your brother deposited him in the house before he went to get my curricle—David went to get it, that is, not Primrose."

Elizabeth's expression lightened markedly. "Is David here? Why didn't he come upstairs with you?"

"He wanted to, but I convinced him to go for the doctor. I wanted to be the one to rescue you." He said the words jokingly, but there was a question in his grey eyes. What was he asking her?

After all the wrongs she had committed against him, she was not certain that she wished to find out. "What will happen to the men after the doctor finishes with them?" she asked, not really caring. She had other concerns.

What is to become of me? Of me without you? her anguished heart cried. But, of course, she could not express such thoughts.

Lord Darvey said, "Never mind them, Elizabeth, especially Barton Brimmer. I'm through with him and his whole family."

"Through? Why, what do you mean?"

"Fidelia Brimmer broke off our engagement last night. In fact, she might be marrying Lord North this very minute."

Here was something else that she was responsible for. After all, it was she who put the thought of marrying Miss Brimmer into Lord North's head. "I am so sorry."

"Sorry?" Lord Darvey repeated in a voice barely above a

whisper as he slumped against her. "I hoped you would be glad."

"Lord Darvey? What is it? Are you going to faint?" But his Lordship did not answer.

"Don't move," she said unnecessarily. "I'll be back in a minute with the doctor. Oh, I do hope he's already here."

A short time later, she returned with David and the doctor, an older man who seemed more irritated than anything else when he viewed Lord Darvey's recumbent body. "What is this," he barked, wagging his thick, untidy grey eyebrows, "a charnel house? Are you responsible in some way for this carnage, young lady?"

"Yes, I am," said Elizabeth, her ripe lower lip quivering.

"Don't pay her any mind," said David angrily. "She's hysterical and doesn't know what she's talking about. Of course, she has nothing to do with this. She's my sister, and we were passing by more or less."

The doctor gave David a disbelieving look, but then he turned his attention to his patient. "This material will have to be cut away," he said, lifting a bit of Lord Darvey's blood-stained blue coat. "Young man, I'll need your assistance."

Willing herself to be strong, Elizabeth asked, "Will his Lordship mend? Can't I do anything to help?"

Busy with his patient, the doctor did not even look up. "He'll be fine," he said gruffly. "I doubt the wound is very deep, though he's lost blood. And, no, you can't. In fact, it's not fitting for you to be here. Why don't you be a good girl and wait downstairs?"

Feeling too exhausted to argue, Elizabeth walked to the ground floor as she'd been told. However, she did not enter the drawing room. She had no wish to see her abductors.

She made her way out-of-doors and looked about her at the landscape, which was slowly awakening to the blandishments of spring. The vista with its bits of scattered green brought no joy to her heart. Nor did the sound of robins chirping as they toiled to construct their nests. You had better get used to feeling empty, she told herself mercilessly. That is how it is going to be.

She had to accept reality and get on with her life. In fact, there was no reason to wait in this place now that she knew Lord Darvey would be all right. David would take his Lordship back to London in the curricle, and other hands would minister to him. What possible use was it, except to indulge herself, to see him one more time?

She looked down at her old brown half-boots. They were sturdy enough for the nine-mile walk to Epsom, not an impossible distance for one who was used to country living. She would complete her journey by herself.

She considered leaving a message for his Lordship, but she could not bring herself to do it. He had not told her he loved her. He had not even told her that he forgave her. It was obvious that there was no more to be said.

Instead, she left a terse note for David asking him to say farewell for her to Lady Treadway and to bring Primrose to Epsom as soon as he could. Then, putting one foot determinedly before the other, she set out to return to her uncle's house.

She was almost sorry when a farm cart went by and the driver offered her a ride to her destination. True, her boots had got all wet and muddy, but her exertions had stirred her blood and raised her spirits a little in the process.

Seeing her uncle again dispelled any lingering beneficial effects, of course. Nor did her unannounced appearance seem to do a great deal of good for him. Elizabeth had forgotten how red Lord Beowulf's face could become when he was moved by choler.

"You," he said in accents of loathing and stamped his foot so hard it made two of the skulls on his scarred, old laboratory table topple over. "Judas, traitor, serpent nurtured in my bosom."

"You omitted apostate," Elizabeth said wearily.

"I was getting to that. What do you want?"

Elizabeth wiped the dust from one of the unmatched

mahogany chairs and sat down across from him. "Never fear. I mean only to collect a few things while I wait for David. Once he returns from London, I shall be on my way again."

"Is that so?" Lord Beowulf tugged pettishly at a lock of his thinning red hair. "I hope you do not think that your brother is entitled to the letter of recommendation I wrote. I expect you to destroy it, missy."

Elizabeth's fine brows set belligerently above her eyes. "Indeed, I won't. I earned it by spying on Lord Darvey."

"Spying, is it?" Lord Beowulf glared at her. "Probably none of the things you told me were true."

"They were until you stole Lord Darvey's paper. No, Uncle, as far as I'm concerned I earned that letter, and I mean for David to use it to secure our future. I wouldn't advise you to stand in our way. I'm capable of dangerous behavior, you know."

Lord Beowulf was obviously taken aback. "What's that you say? I'm sure you never were that sort of unnatural female before. That trait must be something you took on from your lover."

"If by lover you mean Lord Darvey, you're out there," Elizabeth said in a curiously detached tone as though she hadn't just been grossly slandered. In truth, she was too wrapped up in wishing that his Lordship *had* been her lover to be angry. At least she would have been left with memories that were more graphic than those she had now.

"Then why would you have helped him instead of me when you know that my theory is the one true one?" Lord Beowulf seemed genuinely puzzled.

What was the use? "Never mind, Uncle; you wouldn't understand. Now, if you have nothing further to say to me, I'm going to my room."

Lord Beowulf's attempt at an ingratiating smile put Elizabeth on her guard. "As a matter of fact, I do have something more to say. You know, my housekeeper left me."

"Do you mean the woman I got from the village? I'm surprised; she seemed a dependable sort."

"Well, she wasn't. Nor was the one who came after her. What I'm saying, Elizabeth, is that I might find it in me to forgive you for what you did if you went back to being housekeeper and David stayed on as well—with the same financial arrangement, of course."

"How generous. Your heart always was larger than your purse." Seeing him nod in agreement, Elizabeth grimaced. She should have remembered that it was pointless to use sarcasm on her uncle; it invariably escaped him.

Still, though it was outrageous, she might accept his offer until David got a place. She looked about the workroom. Never in good array for as long as she could remember, the laboratory looked particularly moth-eaten and untidy now. She would be taking on a great deal, she could see. But at least she'd have something with which to occupy herself.

Several days after her return, she was interrupted at her labors by the arrival into her uncle's small, bleak sitting room of David, Lady Thea carrying Primrose's cage, Lady Palmer, and two maids. None of them seemed in good spirits.

"Is something amiss?" asked Elizabeth redundantly after greeting the gloomy group. "Is it Lord Darvey?"

"Darvey?" David's narrow, handsome face was marred by a scowl. "What does he have to do with anything? He stopped off in the village but will be here soon enough, I suppose."

In response to this news, Elizabeth hastily took off her large brown holland apron and poked frantically at her auburn curls. "Coming here? I would not think he would."

"Whyever not? His wound is healing well; it's no impediment to him."

"I just did not think that he would, not after I . . . and not after Uncle. . . . Dear me." Collapsing into an ancient curved-leg walnut chair, she absentmindedly helped

herself to a long swallow of her uncle's port, a shockingly
unfeminine thing she would never have done if she'd been
less agitated.

She was brought back to herself by Primrose shrilling his
displeasure. Guiltily, she released him from his cage, then
let him run up her arm to her shoulder. This action turned
out to be a mistake from her point of view because it
enabled him to subject her to an earful of pent-up criticisms
and complaints.

At least he was expressing himself, she thought. The
human inhabitants of the room weren't.

Refraining from apologizing for the appearance of the
house only with the greatest effort, she gave directions to
the lone footman for the placement of everyone's baggage.
"I don't think I'll have any tea," whispered Lady Palmer,
making Elizabeth blush to realize that she hadn't offered her
any. "Quarrels unsettle my digestion. If you will excuse
me, I believe I will go to my room now."

David and Lady Thea chose to remain with Elizabeth,
though neither of them seemed to wish to converse with her.
She focused on their white, set faces. So they had been
arguing, had they? Given what a disaster she'd made of her
own life, it was absurd to think she could do them any good.
Still, she felt she had to make the effort.

"Would you like to talk about what is troubling you?" she
asked gently. "Sometimes that helps, and I'd be most
pleased to listen."

David's *no* and Lady Thea's *yes* crossed each other. The
two, sitting at opposite ends of the same lumpy brown
brocade sofa, pokered up even more.

"What is it?" Elizabeth ignored her uncooperative
brother to ask Lady Thea.

"Everything. When I suggested to this exasperating man
that we wed, he turned me down."

"You did? Did he really?"

Looking vexed to ribbons, David said, "Of course, I did.
I'm not going to marry any woman until I can support her

properly. I am certainly not going to marry a *rich* woman—" he said the word with loathing—"until I can
support her in the manner to which she's accustomed,
though I doubt I'll ever be able to do that unless I find a
position in an outpost like Jamaica. Therefore, Thea will
just have to wait, maybe forever."

"You see!" The usually stalwart Lady Thea seemed close
to tears. "I've told him that I'll marry no one but him. I've
told him that I have enough of a fortune for us both. I've
said everything there is to say, but he won't listen."

"You don't understand," David said sullenly.

Lady Thea removed her poke-shaped straw bonnet and
settled back on the uncomfortable sofa as though prepared
to sit out a long siege. "Men who are fortune hunters marry
women richer than they all the time. That is why they marry
them. Not that I'm comparing you to a fortune hunter," she
added hastily, apparently realizing that she had said the
worst possible thing.

With suppressed violence, David banged the cushion
between them. "Then you're the only one who won't do
so."

"That is not true." Lady Thea's brown eyes sparkled with
impatience. "My parents approve of you." Since it was
patently obvious to anyone who knew Lady Thea and her
parents that the latter would never dare stand in the way of
their determined daughter, this information was not especially valuable.

Elizabeth sighed. "I'm afraid I don't comprehend why
Lady Thea's fortune is an impediment, either, David.
Would you refuse to marry her if the positions were
reversed?"

"Certainly not. What do you take me for? Don't look at
me with that little smirk, Liz, as though you've trapped me
with something clever. It's a different proposition, because
I am a man. You and Thea don't understand because you
expect to be taken care of. It doesn't make you feel
humiliated when you are."

Elizabeth pushed back her chair and went to stand in front of the fire, where she gazed for a few minutes into the meager flames. Then she turned back to the others. "But David," she said with a little smile, cocking her pretty auburn head at him, "your lack of fortune is easily remedied. All you need do is marry Lady Thea. Then her money will be yours, and you will be rich enough to be a suitable mate for her. Once you are rich, your former lack of funds will be irrelevant."

"What?" David's mouth fell open. "That is the most ridiculous thing I've ever heard. You're about as logical as Uncle Beowulf, sister; in fact, that's exactly the sort of thing he'd say. I hope it isn't catching."

"I hope it is." Elizabeth's green eyes snapped. "Otherwise, you're going to make the two of you very unhappy, not to mention Lady Thea's parents. Is your pride worth a life of misery for four people—and for me as well, David, because I love you and don't want to see you like this?"

When he did not answer, she said more mildly, "You should forget masculine pride, my dear. That game isn't worth the candle."

While Elizabeth and Lady Thea watched him anxiously, David paced the room in agitation. Then he walked over to his sister and grasped her hand. "You're right. Well, actually, you aren't right, but what does it matter? I'll be a good husband, and I'll take care of the family's properties as though they had been mine from the start. Best of all, I'll love Thea with my whole heart—except for the part I save for you. Thank you, Liz." Leaning over, he kissed her. Then he went to his beloved and put out his arms.

Elizabeth had no wish to play gooseberry, not that the enthralled couple would have noticed if she'd discarded her dress directly in front of them. She shooed her tiny pet into his cage, then took herself and him out of the room.

"It's for the best, Primrose," she said in a voice from which she could not quite keep out the sorrow. She had lost Lord Darvey, not that she'd ever truly had him, and now she was losing her brother. It was difficult not to feel sorrow. "Thank goodness, I still have you, though. We'll muddle through."

"I think there's been enough muddling," a forceful, well-loved voice said. Lord Darvey's hand clamped around her wrist. "You weren't planning to go anywhere, were you? I shan't let you run off again."

Elizabeth blushed with shame. "I didn't want to the last time, but the doctor said that you would be all right, and I knew you would never forgive me. I saw no point in prolonging matters."

"I'll give you a point!" said Lord Darvey, taking Primrose's cage from her and setting it down. "I love you." Then he proceeded to kiss Elizabeth with the extreme thoroughness of a man of science.

When she was finally able to talk once more, she said shyly, "I do not understand. Aren't you angry with me for lying to you—and all of the other things I did?" She let her voice trail off into vagueness, having decided to forego enumerating the remainder of her crimes.

Lord Darvey looked about the dark hallway with its dingy plaster walls as though anger were a tangible thing to be sought out and located. "No," he said easily, lowering his compellingly handsome face to hers, "I appear not to be. Only the love is left; I seem to have lost the anger."

"What are you doing here, you viper?" roared Lord Beowulf, who must have found the lost emotion. "How dare you come to my house!"

"I had no choice. You have something here that belongs to me."

Lord Beowulf shifted uneasily, his outrage tinged now with anxiety. "If you mean that paper of yours that was stolen, I deny taking it. Besides, you didn't need it. You managed to give a report to the Royal Society without it—not that what you read wasn't a parcel of nonsense."

"Likely the entire subject is," Lord Darvey stated amiably. "At least it seems so to me after talking with your rector."

"The rector!" Lord Beowulf put back his shiny, nearly bald head and laughed. "What does he know about skulls?"

Lord Darvey's grey eyes crinkled at the corners with amusement. "He knows about one. We've been corresponding about it for some little time now, and today I went to see it. It is very large, the largest human skull I've ever seen, in fact."

"Is that so? And it belonged to an Englishman, didn't it?" Lord Beowulf said smugly. "It must have if the rector had it. How did he get it, by the way?"

"I believe it was exhumed by grave robbers at the cemetery attached to the church. He caught them at their work."

"The meddler!" Lord Beowulf said disapprovingly. "But at least he must have seen to whom the skull belonged. There are several men of noble birth buried there. I wonder which one of them it was."

Lord Darvey grinned. "Not any, I'm afraid. The skull came from a member of the lower orders, a milkmaid, I believe. Oh, yes, and the rector said that she was an idiot."

His Lordship and Elizabeth watched in fascination as her uncle's face went from pink to cherry to deepest scarlet. "What's that you say? A female, and an idiot? I don't believe it."

Lord Darvey laughed. "I didn't think you would."

Elizabeth sat on Justin Darvey's lap in a dim corner of the drawing room. Her dress was pushed off her shoulders and Darvey's lips toured hotly over her skin. "Where is this leading?" thought Elizabeth dizzily, then blushed when she felt his Lordship's hand slide down and answer her question.

This was hardly the place for such an activity. Anyone could come walking in. "Ah . . . uh . . . are you comfortable, my lord?" she asked tremulously in an effort to distract him.

Lord Darvey's handsome, dark head came up. "What?"

"I asked if you were comfortable. It is a bit cold."

"Is it?" He straightened and let his grey eyes sweep over her exposed skin. "Yes, I can see why you might think so, my dear," he said with a crooked grin. "Here, let me help you."

He started to tug at her bodice but then seemed to forget what he was supposed to be doing. His hands began to explore her again. Elizabeth had not taken into account how single-minded he could be when something truly interested him.

She cast about for a subject that might engage him more than the last. Grasping both his hands, she asked, "Was what you told Uncle about that grand specimen really true?"

"Specimen?" He seemed to pull himself back from a great distance. "Oh, yes, the specimen. Do you doubt me?" His Lordship tapped the end of Elizabeth's small nose with his finger. "And we not even married yet." When she looked about to apologize, he said, "It is true, but when I told your uncle, I knew he wouldn't believe it. As for me, I'm rather pleased I found it out; it affords me one more reason to give up the study of skulls."

"You can't do that," Elizabeth protested. "You wouldn't be the same person if you weren't a natural philosopher."

Lord Darvey's white teeth flashed. "Did I say I intended to give up natural philosophy? I mean to find something else to study, that is all. And as for being the same person, I haven't been that since I met you. Once I used to be a rational, logical man, you know."

"I agree it isn't rational for you to want me after what Uncle and I have done to you," Elizabeth said in a muted voice. "I still cannot believe that you do."

"Give yourself a decade or so," Lord Darvey advised with mock seriousness. "You will. As for logic, I've found it only takes one so far. It doesn't seem to have a great deal to do with love. Don't talk any more now, Elizabeth. Kiss me."

Some time later, as they were preparing to quit the room and go in search of the other pair of lovers, Elizabeth said musingly, "I wonder what pursuit you'll take up next."

"I didn't think I should mention it before," Lord Darvey said with a quirky little smile, "but I already know what it will be. I plan to study beetles."

Elizabeth's lovely face, deliciously pink from Lord Darvey's kisses, paled to an ashy white. "Oh, no, not beetles; you cannot mean it."

"And why not, may I ask?"

"Because beetles are vastly ugly and I am afraid of them. Don't you remember that night in the kitchen when I jumped onto your shoes to escape them?"

Lord Darvey laughed. "Indeed, I do. That is one of the reasons I chose them; I like it when you fling yourself at me. The other reason is your tendency to violence."

"Violence? I?"

"Certainly. Was it not you who broke Lord Herbert's leg using my lead shot? With beetles I'll have no cause for alarm. It's only with the greatest difficulty that one can manage to throw them. I know; I did an experiment."

Although Elizabeth laughed, she waited uncomfortably for him to bring up as further proof of her violent nature the fact that she had stabbed him. Instead, he only smiled at her, the cool grey eyes lit by love.

Elizabeth caught her breath.

"Oh, very well, my dearest lord; beetles it shall be."

From the *New York Times* bestselling author
of <u>Morning Glory</u> and <u>Bitter Sweet</u>

LaVyrle Spencer

One of today's best-loved authors of bittersweet human drama and captivating romance.

___THE ENDEARMENT	0-515-10396-9/$4.95
___SPRING FANCY	0-515-10122-2/$4.50
___YEARS	0-515-08489-1/$4.95
___SEPARATE BEDS	0-515-09037-9/$4.95
___HUMMINGBIRD	0-515-09160-X/$4.95
___A HEART SPEAKS	0-515-09039-5/$4.95
___THE GAMBLE	0-515-08901-X/$4.95
___VOWS	0-515-09477-3/$5.50
___THE HELLION	0-515-09951-1/$4.95
___TWICE LOVED	0-515-09065-4/$5.50
___MORNING GLORY	0-515-10263-6/$5.50
___BITTER SWEET (March '91)	0-515-10521-X/$5.95
